Beautifully Broken Pieces

A Small Town Romance

Second Hope Series

Jessica Prince

To every person who ever felt nervous to put up personal boundaries because they didn't want to offend anyone else. It's not wrong or selfish to put yourself first. You've earned it.

Let's Connect

By signing up for my newsletter, you're guaranteeing you'll stay up to date on all new releases, cover reveals, giveaways, sales, and all the other exciting book news I have coming!

I pinky-promise to use my emails for good only, not to spam you, and make sure each one is enjoyable for everybody.

Sign up on my website at: www.authorjessicaprince.com

A Note from the Author

We've reached the end of the Second Hope series, and while I'm sad to say goodbye, if you know me or have read my books, you know goodbye isn't forever.

Thank you so much for sticking with me on this journey. This series is incredibly special to me. These characters have come to feel like family, and your love for them means the world to me.

Now, I know that some of you are wondering...what about Naomi? What about Hardin? Well, rest assured, just because they didn't get a story in this series doesn't mean they never will. I have big plans for these two, and I can't wait to share what I have up my sleeve.

In the meantime, I hope you enjoy Tanner and Holly's story. Tanner was a new kind of hero for me, full of sweetness and all the golden retriever vibes.

Go forth and enjoy!

Happy reading, and all the love,
    - Jess

Discover Other Books by Jessica

SECOND HOPE SERIES

The Little Things
Tangled Up With You
Twice in a Lifetime
Chasing Forever
Only Ever You
Beautifully Broken Pieces

ASHLAND SERIES

Dead to Rights

WHITECAP SERIES

Crossing the Line
My Perfect Enemy
Turn of the Tides

THE PEMBROOKE SERIES:

Sweet Sunshine
Coming Full Circle
A Broken Soul
Should Have Been Me

WHISKEY DOLLS SERIES

Bombshell
Knockout
Stunner
Seductress
Temptress
Vamp

HOPE VALLEY SERIES:

Out of My League
Come Back Home Again
The Best of Me
Wrong Side of the Tracks
Stay With Me
Out of the Darkness
The Second Time Around
Waiting for Forever
Love to Hate You
Playing for Keeps
When You Least Expect It

Never for Him

REDEMPTION SERIES
Bad Alibi
Crazy Beautiful
Bittersweet
Guilty Pleasure
Wallflower
Blurred Line
Slow Burn
Favorite Mistake
Sweet Spot

THE CLOVERLEAF SERIES
Picking up the Pieces
Rising from the Ashes
Pushing the Boundaries
Worth the Wait

THE COLORS NOVELS
Scattered Colors
Shrinking Violet
Love Hate Relationship
Wildflower

THE LOCKLAINE BOYS

Fire & Ice

Opposites Attract

Almost Perfect

CIVIL CORRUPTION SERIES

Corrupt

Defile

Consume

Ravage

GIRL TALK SERIES:

Seducing Lola

Tempting Sophia

Enticing Daphne

Charming Fiona

STANDALONE TITLES:

One Knight Stand

Chance Encounters

Nightmares from Within

DEADLY LOVE SERIES:

Destructive

Addictive

Chapter One

Tanner

T*hen*

I KNEW what the doctor was going to say before he even came into the room, but that didn't do a damn thing to lessen the nerves twisting my insides into knots as the door to my exam room swung open and Dr. Pendry walked inside.

"Okay, let's just see what's going on here," he muttered as he stuck the X-ray film up on the viewer. I looked down at my lap as I struggled to swallow the lump the size of an avocado pit that had suddenly formed in my throat. I couldn't bring myself to look at that fucking film. I already knew what was on it. The image might as well have spelled out the words *Your Season Is Over* in neon.

"Ah. Just as I suspected. You've suffered an athletic pubalgia."

A goddamn sports hernia. *Fuck my life.*

As the doctor prattled on, saying words like "rehabilitation" and "physical therapy", all I could think about was how my future in the NHL was up in the air. I didn't know what would happen come next season, and I'd just ended this one on a hell of a low note.

As far as injuries went, this was far from the worst. Certainly not a career ender. Hell, I was lucky enough I didn't even need surgery. But seeing as it was coming on February, I was out for what remained of the regular season. Which added insult to the injury since my team, the Rebels, hadn't made it into the playoffs this season.

I sure as shit hadn't helped our chances, given that I'd been playing injured for longer than I should have. Unfortunately, I'd let my pride get in the way of my physical health and look where that had gotten me.

I'd just celebrated my thirty-seventh birthday a few months back, and I sure as hell had been feeling my age and everything I'd put my body through lately. The awful truth—the truth I had refused to see until now—was that I wasn't sure I had another season in me.

There wasn't a day I didn't wake up in pain. I did everything in my power to take care of myself—I ate right, I exercised—but hockey was hard as hell on a person's body. Most guys retired before they got to be as old as I was. But I'd spent the last few years pushing myself even harder than I had when I was a rookie, for Christ's sake. All to show that I could still hold my own with the new kids that came in every season.

And now I was paying for it.

My head was in such a fog that I barely remembered the rest of my appointment. I moved on autopilot as the doctor prattled on about anti-inflammatory meds and instructions on compression and wrapping the injury.

I stepped out of the building and into the frigid cold. Despite the temperature, the streets and sidewalks of D.C. were just as busy as always.

I caught recognition in the eyes of a couple people as I passed. It was damn near impossible not to be recognized in the city when I'd played for their team for so many years and even won them two Stanley Cups. Usually, I appreciated my fans—at least the ones who weren't assholes any time we lost—but I wasn't in the mood today. I didn't feel like stopping for selfies or to sign whatever they had on hand, so I kept my gaze down and pulled the hood of my sweatshirt up in a pathetic attempt to hide my identity.

D.C. had been home to me for years. I loved the city, but with the news I just received, I felt like the walls were closing in on me. I needed to get the hell out of here. Go somewhere where people didn't know who I was—or at the very least, didn't give a damn.

I hunched my shoulders, trying to burrow deeper into my hoodie and coat as I moved down the sidewalk toward my condo, pushing the pain in my abdomen to the back of my mind. I'd learned a long time ago to compartmentalize. When I was younger, I'd played through injuries worse than this. That was probably why I could no longer bounce back the way I used to.

My cell buzzed continuously in my pocket, but I couldn't bring myself to pull it out. I wasn't in the mood to talk to anyone at the moment.

The doorman of my building greeted me with a nod that I returned as I beelined straight for the elevators. There was an unopened bottle of expensive-as-shit Scotch upstairs that was calling my name. It was supposed to have been for after—once the season had ended. I didn't drink during the season. I needed a clear head at all times if I was going to give my job a hundred percent. But it had become a tradition to crack open a bottle of fine Scotch once it was over to celebrate some much-needed time off.

However, just then, I felt more like drowning my

sorrows. There wasn't much to celebrate with today's news.

"Christ, it's about time you got back. We've been waiting for-fuckin'-ever."

I rolled my eyes at the sound of the intrusive voice and tossed my keys in the bowl I kept on the table just inside the front door.

"Sorry. I didn't realize I have company I needed to hurry for."

I rounded the corner into the large open living space. Sure enough, the assholes I called friends and teammates were hanging out like they owned the place.

The Rebel's left winger, Caleb McClusky, was lounging on my sofa, his feet kicked up on the coffee table as he flipped through one of the many paperbacks littered around my apartment. Our starting center, Mateo Lee was rummaging through my fridge, making himself a huge ass sandwich with what looked like everything I had. Then there was Luke Christof, our center and team captain, sitting at the island. My stack of mail and catalogues I hadn't gone through yet was by his elbow, and it looked like he'd been flipping through it. Not surprising, given how intrusive these fuckers could be when they wanted to.

I was close to all the guys on our team. You had to be in order to do what we did. A team didn't flow right if there was discourse in its ranks. But these three guys were more than just teammates. Hell, they were more than friends. They were my family, and out of all of them, I'd known Luke the longest. I'd been in the league longer than he had, but we'd both joined the Rebels around the same time. I'd stood up as his best man at his wedding, and had been one of the first people to meet their first daughter when she'd been born two years ago.

I headed in the direction of the kitchen, knocking McClusky's feet off my coffee table as I passed. "What are you assholes doing here?" I asked as I snatched the envelope from Luke's fingers and stuffed it and the rest of my unopened mail, into a drawer where he couldn't get at it. *Nosy bastard.* "Shouldn't you be resting up for tonight's game?"

Lee looked at me like I'd grown a second head. "The hell you mean, what are we doing here?"

"Why do you think we're here?" McClusky asked in offense. "We're here to make sure you're okay."

I reached around and rubbed at the tension stiffening the back of my neck. I didn't know how the hell to answer that, mainly because I didn't have the first clue if I was okay or not. So I answered the only way I knew how.

"Season's over for me, boys." I spent the next few

minutes relaying everything I recalled from the doctor's appointment.

The flashes of pity and sympathy in my friends' eyes was all it took to make the walls feel like they were closing in on me, and my three-thousand square foot condo suddenly felt stifling. Was there even air pumping in here?

"Hey, it's not so bad," Lee attempted, his tone placating. "At least you'll be back next season, right?"

Silence filled the room, making the air thick and heavy. I couldn't get the words out. Luckily, I didn't have to, because Luke knew me too damn well. He could practically read what was going through my head.

"You're thinking about retiring." It wasn't voiced as an accusation or a question, but rather a simple fact.

While he looked calm at the realization, McClusky and Lee were anything but. "What?" Lee barked while McClusky snapped, "You've *got* to be kidding me. You can't retire! We need you."

If only that were true.

"I'm thirty-seven, McClusky." Finally speaking those words out loud was physically painful, slicing at my throat like a sheet of sandpaper. "I'm not bouncing back the way I used to."

"You make it sound like you're ancient." Lee crossed

his arms and scowled down at me like I'd pissed him off. "You still have another season or two in you."

The way my knees rattled like rain sticks every damn time I bent them said otherwise. So did the fact it took a good five minutes to get my sore ass out of bed every morning because I had to wait for my muscles to unlock and my joints to loosen.

"You're the best goalie in the whole goddamn league," McClusky insisted, and as much as I wanted to, I couldn't ignore the truth any longer.

"I used to be," I admitted, giving voice to the intrusive thoughts I'd been having for way too goddamn long. "I used to be the best, but I'm not anymore." The stats spoke for themselves. "I'm too goddamn old and tired. I can't keep up with these young kids coming in anymore."

Beneath the sadness and disappointment, I could see understanding in their faces. They knew just as well as I did the toll this job took on our bodies. They were fortunate enough to have less years under their belt than I did. McClusky and Lee were only twenty-five and twenty-six, respectively. Luke, though, was thirty, nearly thirty-one, so he got it more than the other two.

As much as the four of us might have wanted to deny it, I was slowing down. Everyone knew it, but I couldn't shake that small kernel of hope deep inside me that refused to go away.

"Look, I'm not saying it for sure. Nothing's set in stone. Right now I need to focus on healing. And you guys need to focus on tonight's game, not worry about me, okay?"

"I could have sworn I caught McClusky's bottom lip poke out in a pout before he caught himself. "How the hell are we supposed to win another cup without you?"

"Hey, knock that shit off," Luke said firmly. "We'll win another cup because we're that fucking good as a team."

"Damn straight." I nodded in agreement because it was a fact. As much as the devil on my shoulder might want to pretend I was the sole reason for the two cups the Rebels had won, it was because of the work we all put in.

"Amen." Luke nodded resoundingly as he pushed to standing. "That's a consideration for another day. Why don't you take some time away," he suggested as though he was living inside my own brain and could sense what I'd been thinking before I even thought it. "Take a break, you know? Maybe get out of the city and decompress for a bit. Get your head on straight."

That was exactly what I needed. And I was pretty sure I knew the perfect place to go. The one place where I'd felt the calmest in a really long time.

I saw the guys out, wishing them good luck on

tonight's game, then snatched up my phone. I had an open-ended reservation to book.

Chapter Two

Holiday

ow

A FRIGID WIND blew past me as I stepped out of my car, lifting my hair and whipping the strands around so they slapped me in the face. I wasn't sure if it was my mind playing tricks on me, but it seemed unnaturally quiet, the clap of my car door shutting cracking through the still air like a gunshot.

I didn't know why the hell I was doing this. I didn't want to be here, but I couldn't stop thinking about it. So when the thought popped into my head for the thousandth time only seconds after I woke up this morning, I decided that today was the day. I was pulling the trigger on this once and for all, and hopefully, the urge and all thoughts of *him* would finally go away.

I lifted my face to the sky, squinting as the wind pierced my eyes and cheeks, feeling like a million tiny needles puncturing my skin. I couldn't shake the thought that the dull gray sky was fitting, as were the bare trees, with their gnarled, twisted limbs. Given what I was about to do, the dreary day matched my current mood.

The dead, frost-coated grass crunched beneath my boots with each hesitant step I took. I passed headstones of all different shapes and sizes, all of them having one thing in common—the one thing that was missing from the headstone I sought out. Etched into each stone were proclamations of love. How much the person buried beneath the ground was missed greatly by their family and friends.

When I finally reached my destination, I stuffed my hands into the pockets of my coat and looked down at the basic marker, void of any frills or mentions of love. All that had been carved into this one was a name and two numbers. The year he was born, and the year he died. That was it. Since the cost was per letter, we'd decided to put the very minimum. We didn't even put specific dates.

Daniel Bradbury
1953-2025

That was what my siblings and I had agreed on as a family. My brothers, Rhodes and Raylan, had argued that we shouldn't even give him that. But my oldest sister, Gypsy, the woman who had been responsible for raising all of us, couldn't bring herself to leave him to the county to be cremated and dumped wherever they saw fit.

Even if that was all he'd deserved from us.

Her heart was too good, despite having come from two of the most heartless people on the planet. All the good in me and my siblings was solely due to her.

When she let us know what she intended to do, we'd all insisted on splitting the cost. There was no way in hell we were going to let her bury the man who was our father due to biology alone by herself. But we put our foot down when she started talking about a funeral. As far as any of us were concerned, he hadn't done a single thing in his life to earn us honoring him in death. It had been a random Tuesday, one I hadn't even bothered to take off work, when Danny Bradbury had been laid to rest without a single person, aside from the grounds workers, to stand by and watch as the cheapest casket the funeral home had in stock was lowered into a hole in the ground.

While the headstones all around his were adorned with flowers and other keepsakes, Danny's had nothing. I wasn't surprised. I didn't think any of my brothers or sisters had been out here since we picked the spot. This was certainly a first for me. And if I had any say in the matter, it was also the last.

I didn't know what I expected to feel as I stared at my father's headstone, my eyes tracing over each letter and number. I wasn't here out of obligation as his daughter. I wasn't here because I missed him. After all, how could you miss a person you didn't know. I was only a toddler when he and our mother, Peggy, had taken off, and even when they were there, they didn't do much rearing. They popped out kids then left their oldest to raise them. Gypsy had taken responsibility for us from the moment we came into this world. She cleaned our scrapes and held us if we woke up from a nightmare. She packed our lunches and read us bedtime stories every night.

I never felt like I was missing anything by not having a mother around, because my oldest sister was all the mother I could possibly need. And when her husband Marco came into the picture, he slotted right into the role of father.

So, no. I didn't miss Danny Bradbury. Not one bit. But I couldn't shake the sadness I felt at the thought of how he died. I might not have liked the man—in fact, I didn't feel much of anything for him—but he'd died alone. No one to worry or care or hold him if he was scared. And that was just . . . sad.

I guess the feeling that had been plaguing me ever since Gypsy called a family meeting to tell us what had happened all those months ago was pity. It was pity that pulled me out here on a cold, dreary day when I would have loved nothing more than to stay inside, curled up with a book.

I inhaled deeply, pulling the cold air into my lungs until it caused them to burn before blowing it out on a cleansing exhale.

"I feel like I should talk instead of just standing here, but I don't know what to say," I admitted to the lifeless piece of stone. "I don't miss you. You won't get that from me. You won't get that from any of us."

I thought back to what Raylan had told us shortly after we laid our father to rest. To the memory he'd held onto for years all by himself. How he'd run into our father out of the blue, and how his last words to him had been heartless and cruel, leaving my brother to think the worst of himself. He knew better now. He'd shaken that darkness off, thanks to the help of his girlfriend and my best friend, Lennix

Paulson. But after hearing that, I knew without a shadow of a doubt the words I'd just spoken to Danny were true.

"I guess . . . I guess I'm just sorry you were all alone when you died. I wouldn't wish that on anyone. Even you. My hope for you was that it was fast, that you felt no fear, because I wouldn't want something like that on my worst enemy."

The fist that felt like it had been clutching my chest for the past few months finally began to loosen as I let the words out, so I kept going, saying the last words I ever intended to say to Danny Bradbury before I moved on with my life for good. "I hope you've found whatever peace you lacked in life that made you such an unhappy person."

With those last words, I finally felt some of the peace *I'd* been lacking lately fall into place. I hadn't forgiven or forgotten, but I had gotten some form of closure with this visit, and that was enough for me.

I felt lighter as I headed back to my car, ready to put this whole morning behind me. I'd just started the engine when my cellphone chirped from where I'd kept it stashed in the cupholder while I'd been out in the cemetery.

I picked it up, my stomach plummeting to the ground as I scanned the text that had come in a few minutes earlier. The number came up as unknown, but that was only because I hadn't saved it in my contacts. I'd refused. But I knew all too well who it was from.

UNKNOWN CALLER:
You can't ignore me forever.

Like hell I couldn't. An indelicate snort rattled up my throat as I tossed the phone back into the cupholder without bothering to respond. In the back of my mind, I knew I should have blocked her number a long time ago, but there was a reason I couldn't. However, that didn't mean I had to feed into her bullshit. And that was the last thing I intended to do, at least for now. My morning had been gloomy enough. I was determined to find the sunshine.

THE BELL above the door chimed, soft and beautiful. I looked over from the customer I was helping and smiled as my oldest sister stepped inside.

"Hey," I greeted with a big smile. "Give me just a second."

Gypsy gave me a nod and headed deeper into the store.

I finished ringing up my customer, sliding her books into a bag with my store's logo on the front, and passed it over to her with a smile. "Hope you enjoy it. Let me know what you think of that thriller."

The middle-aged woman grinned, hugging her new purchases to her chest. "Oh, I certainly will."

I would never get tired of hearing that, or seeing the excitement in people's faces whenever they stumbled onto a book that called to them. I'd opened my little independent bookstore, One More Chapter, because I loved to read. Love might not have been a strong enough word. I'd had my nose stuffed in a book ever since I was old enough to read. In fact, the name came from how many times I'd pled with Gypsy to just let me read one more chapter before I had to go to bed.

It took me a while to figure out what I wanted to do with my life and how I could incorporate my love of books into it, but now that I'd opened my shop, I couldn't imagine doing anything else.

It really was true, what people said. I loved my job and my bookstore so much, it never felt like work. The familiar smells of the books made my chest feel lighter. The rows and rows of shelves that filled the space surrounded me like a welcoming hug.

It was my happy place, and just walking through the doors was enough to wash away everything from earlier that morning.

I lucked out on the location. The building was in the heart of Hope Valley, a few blocks from the town square, with all its shops and boutiques, and less than a block from the town's most popular coffee shop, Muffin Top. It was prime real estate. The proximity to Muffin Top alone was worth what I paid for it. In the early days, being so close to the coffee shop guaranteed foot traffic. People passed by and came in simply out of curiosity, coffee and pastries in hand. That had given One More Chapter the chance it needed to stand on its own.

I had picked out absolutely every aspect of my shop from the feminine, swirling script on the sign, the tranquil color on the walls, the plush reading chairs scattered throughout so customers could enjoy their books, to the window boxes I kept filled with brightly colored flowers spring through fall. Every inch of it was me, through and through.

Once the customer left, I moved to the door, flipping the sign over that read: *Closed for Book Club*.

I found my sister near the back, in the space I used for gatherings or events, setting up for the monthly book club she'd started with her friends about a year back. These were the women who had been a huge part of my upbringing. My sister's circle was so much more than friends. They were family. They'd been there for me and my siblings for as long as I could remember, and this family that we had built—that Gypsy had created for us —was more special than the families a lot of people were born into, myself included.

There was Eden and Nona, Temperence, but we called her Tempie. She'd been the one to wipe my tears and cast my arm when I'd broken it at six years old. Then there was my best friend Lennix's mother, Rory, along with Sage and Danika. Dani was the one to open Muffin Top years ago, and it was now being run by her step-daughter and another close friend of mine, Macie. Tessa was the director of Hope House, the group home Rory and her husband had started more than two decades ago. And finally, rounding out the menagerie of crazies were Hayden, Charlotte, Stella, and her sister Serenity.

All of the women were married, and a lot had kids of their own, making our chosen family that much bigger.

"So, are you going to tell me how it went, or do you want me to pretend it didn't happen?"

I let out a sigh as I placed a sleeve of plastic cups beside the bottles of wine and charcutrie that Gypsy had already laid out. She was the only one I'd told about my visit to the cemetery before I made it. The only one I talked to about the strange obligation I felt. I wasn't sure my other siblings would have understood. Everyone had their own reaction to Danny Bradbury's death.

"It went. There's really not much else to say."

Gypsy's hand came down on mine, staying my movement and drawing my attention to her face. Her expression was one of understanding and sympathy. "Did you at least find what you needed?"

I nodded, offering her a small, sincere smile. "I think so. There's a sense of closure." At least when it came to my father, that was. I didn't tell her about the phone calls and texts, however. I wouldn't tell any of them. It was my way of protecting them after so many years of them protecting me. Carrying the burden of *her* was the least I could do. It kept them clear of her.

"And that's enough for you? If there's anything I can do—"

I twisted my hand so it was palm to palm with hers, closing my fingers and giving her a reassuring squeeze. "I'm good now. I promise," I assured her, wanting to take that weight off her shoulders. No matter how old we got, she never stopped trying to take care of us. "You've done enough, Gypsy. More than." I could tell there was more she wanted to say, to ask, but I managed to divert her attention. "Now let's finish this up before the rest of the crew gets here." A grin pulled at my lips. "You know how crazy they get if there aren't enough snacks and booze."

She rolled her eyes on a snort, knowing I was right. Those women could be downright feral when they were in the mood. And they tended to be in the mood a lot. It was just one of the many reasons I loved them all so damn much.

Chapter Three

Tanner

Hope Valley had seemed like the most logical place to take the time I needed to heal and to get my head together. I'd come for vacation a couple summers back and had fallen in love with the place almost instantly.

It wasn't hard to see what was so great about this small town, especially compared to the city. The air seemed fresher here. Each breath pulled into my lungs was clean, free of pollution. The mountains provided beautiful views all around, free of the concrete and high-rises that were all I could see through the windows of my condo back in D.C.

The only thing that had taken a bit of getting used to

was the quiet. The nights in Hope Valley were so . . . quiet. Tranquil. At least once I'd adjusted to it.

Sure, it would have been great to have countless restaurants on hand to deliver, but so far that was the only thing I was missing from my real life.

Instead of staying at Second Hope Lodge like I had last time, I decided to rent a place in the foothills since I wasn't sure how long I'd be staying. The cabin was like something I could have only imagined, with massive picture windows that provided views of the surrounding forest no matter what room you were in.

The living room had a stone fireplace and buttery leather furniture in rich caramel that felt like a dream when you sunk into it. With the dark furniture and the natural wood on the walls, it was the perfect space to curl up and read, which I'd done a lot the past couple weeks since getting here. In fact, I was quickly running through the stash of books I'd brought with me from home.

My injury was healing nicely, and I was staying on top of my PT, but it helped to get out every once in a while. I'd done a fair bit of hiking, some light jogging since being cleared, and the house I was renting had a gym in the basement I was taking full advantage of— only light weights for the time being, of course.

Today was my first day venturing into town since I

arrived two weeks ago. It was more boredom than anything else that drove me out into the cold weather. As incredible as the rental cabin was, I could only hole up between those four walls for so long before I needed interaction with other people.

I climbed into my Range Rover and made the twenty-minute drive into the heart of Hope Valley. I didn't have a destination in mind, so I parked in the center of town, near an open green space that held a gazebo and clock tower.

I climbed out and walked for a bit, taking everything in. Close to the town square there were shops and boutiques, a salon called Pure Elegance next to what looked like an accounting firm. As I walked farther I passed a historic-looking red brick building that housed a business called Alpha Omega. According to the sign, it was some kind of private investigation firm.

A couple blocks down was a bar and brewery I'd visited a time or two the last time I vacationed here called the Tap Room that had exceptional beer. There was the Evergreen diner and a coffee shop called Muffin Top. The need for caffeine called to me, and I headed in that direction.

My phone started ringing from inside the pocket of my coat as I crossed the street. I waited until I was safely on the sidewalk before pulling it out. The hope that it was Caleb, Luke, or Mateo disappeared when I saw the name on the screen.

My stomach dropped as Sandra's picture flashed across the screen. I'd had a short-lived situationship with her that I'd ended before I'd gotten hurt. We met at the bar my team and I frequented after home games back in D.C. She caught my eye one night, and the two of us got to talking. She'd just ended an engagement and I was solely focused on my career, so we both agreed that neither wanted anything serious. We'd been on the same page . . . at least at first. It hadn't taken long for things to change, though.

It went from random, casual hookups when we both had free time to her calling and texting every day, asking if I wanted to either go to dinner or come over so she could cook for me. We agreed to no sleepovers, but within a couple weeks she was trying to get me to stay the night at her place, or pretending to fall asleep at mine right after sex. The straw that broke the camel's back was when I caught her sneaking pictures of me in my underwear. I called it off then and there. Since then she'd attempted to pull the "concerned friend" card on multiple occasions, offering to be there for me as I healed or to run any errands I needed. I felt like a dick, leaving her messages unanswered, but I'd spelled things out pretty damn clearly when I told her we wouldn't be seeing each other anymore. However she refused to take a hint.

Mateo had called it from the jump. Apparently she was a known puck bunny who had made her way through the younger players, but thought that, given my age, I'd be more likely to settle down and wife her up. I hadn't been interested in doing either of those things.

I hit the button on the side to send the call to voice-mail and stuffed the phone back into my pocket.

A quick look through the large windows showed the place was packed, giving me a moment of pause. Sports journalists had been reporting on me like crazy since my injury had taken me out for the rest of the season. They loved to speculate about whether or not I was coming back. Not that they had the answer because I didn't know my damn self. But the articles had stirred up enough attention that I hadn't been able to walk the streets in D.C. without being bombarded. That was just one of the many reasons I had to get the hell out of there.

I caught recognition in the faces of a few people I passed as I walked from my car to the coffee shop, but instead of asking for selfies or autographs, they simply nodded and smiled politely before going on about their business.

I had to admit, it was a nice change of pace. That was for damn sure.

I pulled the door opened and stepped into Muffin Top, the scent of roasted coffee beans and sugar greeting me and making my stomach rumble, reminding me I hadn't eaten breakfast yet.

"Oh my god. Tanner?"

A brief burst of annoyance flashed through me. Then I turned around and saw who had called my name, and a smile curled my lips. Her name was Ivy. I'd met her when I visited a couple summers back. She worked at the lodge where I was vacationing, and there had been an immediate attraction. At least on my end. I'd asked her out, even attended the wedding of her friends as her guest. Turned out, we made better friends than anything else. Mainly because she was hung up on another guy and trying to get over him by accepting my request for a date.

"No way! It is you." I opened my arms, and she walked right into them, giving me a brief squeeze before stepping back, smiling up at me warmly. "I had no idea you were here. Are you at the lodge again?"

"Not this time. My trip this time is a little open-ended, so I rented a place. You look incredible."

She beamed happily. "Thanks. Motherhood's really been agreeing with me."

My eyes widened in shock as a tall man in faded jeans, dusty boots, and a thick canvas jacket moved beside her. I recognized him from my last visit, but back then, he hadn't had a tiny baby strapped into a carrier on his chest. I could only assume he was the guy Ivy had been torn up about, and the baby he was holding was theirs.

"Tanner Fine," the guy said in greeting before hooking his arm over Ivy's shoulder and pulling her into his side, all while patting the back of the baby in the carrier. "Good to have you back in town." From the look on his face, I wasn't sure he really meant that, not that I could blame him. But he held his hand out for me to shake anyway. I had to respect the man for that. I wasn't sure I could do the same if I came face to face with a man who pursued and made out with my woman.

"Thanks." I dug through my memories to pull up his name. "It's Connor, right?"

Any lingering uncertainty or animosity melted from his face. His eyes widened slightly and the tips of his ears grew pink. "Uh . . . yeah. Yeah. It's Connor. Man, I can't believe you remember that. That's so cool," he finished on a whisper, a goofy grin taking over his face.

I'd always been really good with names, but I was especially good at remembering the names of my fans, and I recalled this dude nearly swallowing his tongue the first time he saw me back at Second Hope Lodge.

Ivy rolled her eyes good naturedly. "All right. Down,

fan boy." Connor shot her a scowl that made me chuckle. "Tanner, you remember my husband. This is our little girl, Sylvie." She reached over, and with the gentlest smile on her face, trailed a finger over the baby's downy head.

I leaned a little closer for a better look. The tuft of hair on her head was the same light red as her mother's, and long, sweeping lashes were lying across chubby pink cheeks as she slept against her dad's chest. The little cutie's fist was balled up near her mouth like she'd been chewing on it right before conking out. I'd always been so focused on my career that I never really gave the whole family thing much thought. At least until my buddy Luke's baby was born.

I had to admit, that day had brought a sense of longing to the surface I'd never been able to fully stuff back down. And seeing Ivy's daughter, bundled up in her fluffy pink winter wear, was like throwing Miracle Grow on that little bloom Luke's family had given life to. "Congratulations, you guys," I said softly, not wanting to wake her up despite the noisy café around us. "She's beautiful."

The expression on Connor's face as he stared down at his daughter could only be described with one word. Adoration. And I'd be damned if it didn't send a spike of envy through my chest. I did my best to shake the sensation off. Babies and marriage were the last thing I needed to be thinking about, especially with everything being so damn uncertain.

"Thanks," Ivy said with a smile. "So, what brings you to town?" Her brows pulled together in confusion. "You can't be on vacation . . ."

"Butterfly," Connor said quietly, but I didn't miss the gentle warning in his tone. Meaning he already knew about the injury.

"It's okay," I assured him before looking back at Ivy. "I actually am on vacation. An injury took me out for the remainder of the season, but I'm okay now."

"I'm really sorry," she offered genuinely, reminding me how sweet she'd been. It was one of the reasons I'd asked her out in the first place. But seeing her now, with her beautiful daughter and a husband who was so clearly devoted to them both, there wasn't a doubt that things had worked out exactly how they should have. This family was exactly what she deserved, and I was beyond happy for her.

"But, hey, there's a silver lining." I arched a brow in silent question. "You're here," she said excitedly. "And this is the best place in the whole world. I mean, we might not have as much to offer as a big city, but at least we don't have traffic jams and city noise and rude strangers."

She had me there. I chuckled, "It is a pretty great place. And I'm sure once I find my way around I'll like it even more. That's actually why I'm out today. Just scoping the place out. I need to get familiar with the town. You know, find where to get my groceries, coffee . . ." I waved my hand around the coffee shop in indication. "Stuff like that."

Connor spoke up then. "As far as coffee and pastries goes, you won't get better than this place. Trust me. And we're happy to point you wherever else you need to go."

"Actually, if you could point me in the direction of a bookstore, that would be great. I've read pretty much everything I brought with me already."

Ivy's face lit up. "Of course! My friend Holly owns a place right down the block. It's called One More Chapter. Just head left out the door and you can't miss it."

"Thanks. I appreciate that."

"Anything you need, don't hesitate to let us know. And we need to have you over one night for dinner."

"I'd love that," I said, finding that I really meant it. It would be nice to have people to hang out with while I was here. The guys FaceTimed me regularly to keep in touch, but it wasn't the same as having them with me.

We said our goodbyes a minute later, and I headed to the counter to order coffee and a slice of banana bread. Since I was out, I didn't have to watch my diet as strictly as if I were still playing. So if I wanted sugar, I was damn well going to have it.

With my coffee in one hand and a white paper bag with my pastry in the other, I headed out the door back into the cold, taking a left like Ivy instructed.

"Holy shit," I mumbled to myself after my first sip. Connor had been right; the coffee was amazing. Maybe the best I'd ever had.

That was definitely a mark in the pro column for Hope Valley.

Chapter Four

Holiday

"Ooh, what about this guy?"

I didn't bother looking up from my task of unboxing a shipment of new books to acknowledge the phone my friend Naomi was waving in front of my face.

"Pass."

"But you didn't even look," she said with a pout.

I was sure the man in the picture she was so eagerly trying to show me was handsome—Naomi had good taste, and all that—but it didn't matter if he was the sexiest man on two legs. "I don't need to look. The answer is always going to be no."

She let out a disgruntled huff, dramatically tossing herself back in the plush chair closest to where I was currently working. "You're no fun at all. Online dating is totally safe."

"It's not the online part of it that I'm opposed to."

Ever the drama queen, Naomi crossed her eyes and blew out an obnoxious raspberry. "Boo. You're no fun," she declared as she clicked out of the dating app she'd been scrolling through and shifted in the chair to stuff her phone into her back pocket.

I smiled, unable to help myself. Naomi Sheppard's craziness was just one of the reasons we all loved her so damn much. Gypsy liked to joke that Naomi's wild streak was a gift from Karma to test her father, Lincoln. And to hear her mother, Eden, tell it, she was responsible for every single gray hair on her father's head.

"Shouldn't you be at work right now?"

She lifted her shoulder in a careless shrug and threw a leg over the arm of her chair like she was settling in. "Ugh. I'm taking a mental health break. If I don't, I'm liable to beat one of those pains in my ass senseless." Her eyes came to mine. "No offense. I know your brother is technically my boss."

Naomi had made a career at her father's company, Alpha Omega, coming in to wrangle the men who worked there when the previous woman who held her position, Roxanne, retired a few years back. When

Lincoln decided to retire for good, he'd handed the business over to my oldest brother, Rhodes.

"No offense taken. I grew up with him, remember? So I know exactly how punchable his face can be at times."

She pointed her finger at my face. "See? You get it. Now, back to this whole dating thing . . ."

My head fell back on my shoulders as I groaned up at the ceiling. "Are we really back on this? I told you, I'm taking a break from dating."

"Come on. You can't just give up because of a couple lousy relationships."

I snorted, shooting her a look of disbelief. "A *couple* lousy relationships? Are you forgetting about Gregory?"

She pulled her lips into a wince. "Okay yeah. He wasn't so great."

"Not so great? Naomi, he stole my underwear! And not for the reason you'd think." My brows pulled into a frown. "He stretched four pairs to hell. And they were my expensive lacy ones too. Not laundry day panties."

As much money as that jerk had cost me in replacement undergarments, he still wasn't the worst. I'd dated men who gaslit, attempted to cut me off from my family and friends, verbal abusers, and rounding out the suckfest was my last boyfriend, Blane, a manipulative cheater.

If there was a loser out there, it seemed they were drawn right to me. And my radar on spotting them was seriously defective.

As if reading my mind and knowing exactly who I was thinking about, Naomi let out a noise of disgust. "Ugh, *Blane*." She said it with the same passion someone might say *Ugh, I stepped in dog crap.* "Should have known the bastard was evil, based on his name alone. I mean, who's named *Blane*? What is he, the high school bully in every eighties movie ever made?"

I really wished she didn't have a point, but sadly, she was right. I thought I'd been so careful when it came to him. Having been burned one too many times in the past, I'd insisted on taking things slow when we were starting out. He'd been so supportive and understanding that he tricked me into thinking I'd finally landed a good one, a man I could have a future with. Then I showed up at his house one evening with chicken soup because he told me he was sick. Turned out, it wasn't so much the flu he'd come down with as another woman going down on *him*.

The door to the shop was pushed open right then, setting off the gentle bell. I glanced up with a smile that quickly fell from my face at the sight of who'd just walked into my sanctuary.

"Holiday, hi," the venous woman chirped way too brightly.

The sound of my name coming out of her mouth was grating, like nails on a chalkboard. The only people who used my full name were those who barely knew me. And this vicious bitch, of course. "Rebecca," I offered flatly, my tone void of any emotion. I swallowed down the acidic taste in my mouth and forced on a professional mask. "Welcome to One More Chapter."

She looked around the space I'd put so much time and effort into. "I've never been in here before. It's just so . . . quaint."

"Wait. *Rebecca?*" Naomi shot up on her seat, twisting around to give the woman a vicious glower. "You mean the skank you caught on her knees, going to town on that Vienna sausage your ex called a dick?"

I did a terrible job of masking my snort, but did my best to school my features and not laugh at my friend's apt description. I waved her off, silently miming at her to zip her lips before shifting my focus back to the Vienna sausage lover. "What can I help you with, Rebecca?"

She wiped the vicious narrow-eyed glare she was casting Naomi off her face and pasted on a saccharine sweet smile that was fake as hell as she looked back to me. "I was just stopping in to see if you had a section on wedding planning." She held out her hand and wiggled her fingers, causing the diamond on her ring finger to sparkle.

My stomach dropped at the sight of it. Not because I missed him or wanted him back—Rebecca was welcome to the cheating, lying piece of crap—but because, once again, I hadn't been enough for a ring. Or even monogamy, for crying out loud.

"Blane and I are thinking an outdoor ceremony next fall. You know, when the leaves are starting to turn. It'll be so beautiful."

I made it my mission in life to never hate anyone. Hate was like a poison in your bloodstream. But *damn* this woman was making it *really* hard.

"But looking around . . ." She trailed her gaze through my store, curling her top lip up like she found it lacking. *Bitch.* "I'm not sure your little shop will have what I'm looking for."

"You little—" I acted fast, reaching out and placing my hand on Naomi's shoulder and shoving her back down in the chair before she could pounce and scratch Rebecca's eyes out.

"I'm sorry to hear that," I lied through my teeth. "Maybe you'll have more luck in Grapevine or Hidalgo." Any of the surrounding towns *outside* of Hope Valley would work. "But it was nice of you to stop in."

When Naomi pushed to her feet again I didn't

bother trying to stop her. I'd never been good with confrontation, so I was all too happy to leave it to her to usher that she-devil out of my store.

"All right, you human blister, that means it's time to go."

Rebecca let out an affronted huff. "*Excuse* me?"

Naomi continued forward, waving her arms and forcing her to stumble backward toward the door. "You heard me. And just a heads up, you might want to find a new person to do your Botox and filler before the wedding. Your face is starting to look like a Barbie doll after thirty seconds in a microwave."

I couldn't hold my giggle in that time, not that I wanted to. As soon as the door closed behind the wretched woman, I blew out a breath of relief. "Thanks for that."

Naomi turned back to me and crossed her arms over her chest. "You're too nice," she said in a scolding tone.

I moved back to the boxes of books I still had to unpack and display. "I'm not sure there's such a thing as too nice."

Naomi returned to her chair, snatching up one of the copies of the latest romance release I had set up on a special endcap. She flopped down into the seat, sitting sideways with her legs dangling over the arm as she fanned through the pages. "There is when you smile at the vicious bitch your ex cheated on you with instead of snatching the gaudy ring off her finger and chucking it down the storm drain."

"It was gaudy, wasn't it?" I jabbed my finger at her. "And if you break that spine, you're buying that book."

"Already planned on it. Mom's reading it for their book club and wouldn't stop going on about it so I figured I'd see what all the hype was about. And don't think I don't see what you're doing. You're trying to change the subject."

I blew out a sigh. "I don't know what you want me to say. I'm trying to run a business here. I can't just go around alienating anyone who makes me mad. Besides, you know confrontation makes me break out in hives."

Naomi rolled her eyes, but there was no heat behind it. "Fine," she relented grudgingly. "Act like a responsible adult, see if I care."

I shot her a grin. "Thanks for the permission."

"But I still think you need to set up a dating profile." Her hand shot into the air to silence me before I could argue. "At the very least, you need to get laid, because *Blane* can*not* be the last guy you had sex with." She fake shivered like the idea repulsed her, and honestly, given how things had ended between us, I got it. If I could go back in time and undo it all I would. As it was, I'd considered smacking my head into a wall a couple of times in the hopes a brain injury would erase the memory.

"Look, I'm not going to find some random guy to sleep with just so my loser ex is no longer my last." I wasn't opposed to a one-night stand or a casual hookup—not that I'd ever had either—but I wasn't going to search one out either. "That seems a little desperate. I'm off men for the foreseeable future, and that's that."

Naomi gave me a scrutinizing look. "You know, karma's going to get you for that one. For all you know, the next time that door opens it could be the future Mr. Holiday Bradbury waltzing in, and you'd miss out."

My eyebrows lifted toward my hairline. "The future Mr. Holiday Bradbury?"

She lifted a single shoulder in a shrug. "I'm progressive like that."

I let out a laugh at my friend's ridiculousness. "Whatever. I can assure you that the future Mr. anything won't be walking through my door. And I'm fine with that."

I wasn't sure if she'd called on karma personally, but at that very moment, the door swung open, setting off the bells, and the most gorgeous man I'd ever seen—in real life and in pictures—came walking into my shop.

"Holy shit," Naomi whispered, her eyes nearly bulging out of her skull. "I love when I'm right."

Chapter Five

Tanner

The first thing I noticed when I walked into One More Chapter was that the store was downright cozy. With the welcoming colors and comfy seating scattered throughout, it didn't feel like a place where you simply came in to buy books, but where you were welcome to stay, to curl up and read, for as long as you wanted.

The second thing I noticed was *her*.

She was impossible to miss, standing in the middle of the space with all her golden blonde hair hanging down around her shoulders. It was like the sun was shining down on her, spotlighting her beauty.

"Holy shit. I love when I'm right," another woman whispered, drawing my attention to her for the first time. I hadn't noticed her sitting in the chair closest to the woman who'd snagged my attention the moment I walked in.

My lips stretched into a smile as the door closed behind me, my focus stolen once more by the ray of sunshine. "Hi."

Her cheeks flushed and her caramel brown eyes widened. "Uh . . . h-hello." She gaped for a second, her mouth opening and closing like she was struggling to find the right words. The woman in the chair reached up, smacking Sunshine in the stomach lightly like she was trying to snap her out of some sort of daze. Sunshine blinked before clearing her throat and pasting on a tiny, nervous smile. "Welcome to One More Chapter."

"Thanks." I moved closer, taking in the shelves and shelves of books. Then I remembered the coffee cup and pastry bag I was holding from Muffin Top. "Sorry. I'm not sure if you allow outside food—"

She lifted her hand and waved off my concern. Her smile grew a bit wider and brighter, lighting her whole face up and nearly knocking the breath out of my lungs. "Oh, don't worry about it. Muffin Top will always be the exception to any rule."

I let out a low chuckle. "Something I've just learned." I took another sip of the best damn coffee I'd ever hard.

"But if you need to free up your hands, I'm happy to keep your stuff behind the front counter while you shop." She lifted her hands, palms facing outward. "I give you my word it won't be tampered with."

Christ, she was cute. "I trust you." That was something I normally would have to be careful about. I'd learned the hard way there were opportunists around every corner. However, I'd also learned to trust my gut over the years, and my gut was telling me I didn't have anything to worry about where this woman was concerned.

I extended my arms, handing over my coffee and muffin, and watched as she carefully tucked them safely away near the register.

"Thanks, I appreciate it."

"No problem." She seemed more comfortable now that she was focusing on professionalism. "If there's anything else I can help you with, let me know."

She started to turn away from me, but for some reason, the idea of losing those light brown eyes made my stomach drop. I'd dated plenty in my life, probably more than plenty, but I'd never had a reaction like this to a woman before, one where I wanted to keep a complete stranger's attention for as long as possible.

"Actually," I started before she could fully turn

away, "would you mind showing me where you keep your thrillers and murder mysteries?"

"Oh. Yeah, of course."

"Thanks." I gave her a practiced smile that had worked on women in the past and extended my hand to her. "I'm Tanner, by the way."

The apples of her cheeks turned a deep pink and her eyelashes kissed the tops of her cheekbones when she glanced down almost bashfully. And damn if that look didn't do something to me. "Um, yeah. Not to sound creepy or anything, but I know who you are."

I figured by the way she'd looked at me when I first walked in. "You're a hockey fan?"

"Oh, no. Nothing like that." Her eyes flared wide like she was afraid she'd just insulted me. "I mean, I don't *not* like it. I've never really watched it." I raised my brows quizzically, and she lifted her shoulder in a shrug before explaining, "It's a small town, and you were kind of an exciting topic for people last time you were here. Also, I was at the wedding you attended with my friend Ivy."

"Ah. Well, I'm at a massive disadvantage," One corner of my mouth kicked up in a smirk. "You know about me, but I don't know anything about you."

"Oh. Um . . ."

"Jesus, this is painful to watch," her friend muttered

in a whisper that was intentionally loud enough for us to hear. She pushed to her feet, standing a good three inches shorter than Sunshine, if not more. "Tanner, this stunning vision right here is my sweet, kind-hearted, *gorgeous* friend, Holiday Bradbury. But we all call her Holly, so feel free to do the same."

"*Naomi!*" Sunshine—also known as Holly—hissed, her face growing redder and covered in a look of horror.

Naomi bugged her eyes out at her friend. "What?" she whisper-yelled. "Is anything I just said a lie?"

"Don't you have a job you need to get back to?"

Naomi flopped back down in the chair, kicking her legs up over the arm and swinging them from side to side. "Oh, not a chance in hell."

The muscle in Holly's jaw ticked wildly as she mimicked her friend's bug-eyed look, and I got the feeling they were having some sort of silent argument.

"Holiday," I said quietly, breaking into their mental fight. "That's a beautiful name." My eyes locked gazes with hers. "It fits."

Naomi's jaw dropped for a second before she smiled a Cheshire-cat smile. Meanwhile, Holly looked like she wanted to hide away all of a sudden. And something inside me screamed not to let that happen.

"So, the thriller section?" I reminded her before she

could do something like take off running in the opposite direction.

"Right!" Her body jolted back into reality and she gave her head a shake. "I'm so sorry. It's right this way."

I followed after her like a magnet being drawn to its polar opposite. As I trailed behind her, I caught a whiff of her scent, it was like oranges and cloves, warm and sweet with only the slightest hint of spice. It was a scent that reminded me of sunshine, just like her, and I caught myself inhaling deeply to pull more of that smell into my lungs, holding on to it for as long as I could.

"I think you'll find everything you're looking for on these shelves here," she said with a flick of her delicate wrist before turning to face me and giving me a smile that hit me like a punch to the solar plexus. God, she really was beautiful. "If you need anything else, just holler."

"Do you read thrillers, Holiday?" I asked, unable to help myself.

"You can call me Holly. And, yeah. I actually read a little of everything. A *lot* of everything, actually," she answered, and the way her face lit up as she talked about books told me she had a real passion for them. "Reading has been my favorite thing to do basically since I learned how. I read anything."

"I get that. Isn't it the best way to wind down?"

Her eyes sparkled as she nodded excitedly. "It really is. Add in a glass of wine and a bubble bath and we're talking heaven."

A low chuckle rattled my throat. "Oh, that's the only way I read." Her giggle sounded like windchimes. "Do you have any recommendations?"

Her hand came up, her fingers dragging through her long golden hair as her eyes traveled to the side in thought. She hummed as she trailed her fingers across the colorful spines of the books, searching for one she liked. "This one was really good. The twist near the end caught me by surprise. Oh! And this one. It's a little spooky if that's your thing. I'll admit, I was reading this one late at night and it kind of creeped me out a bit. I had to sleep with the lights on."

"I love a good creep out. I'll take both. Anything else?" I followed her like an eager puppy as she spoke passionately about books she enjoyed. In less than ten minutes, I was holding a stack of seven books, and I was fully prepared to buy anything else she liked. Hell, if she'd recommended the phone book I probably would have bought it.

I tucked away for future use the knowledge that talking about books brought Holly out of her shell and made her shine brighter, because I absolutely planned on using it again later. Anything to make her comfortable enough to go on and on the way she was just then.

"I'm sorry," she said on a small laugh. "I didn't mean to talk your ear off. I tend to ramble when it comes to books."

"Please. Don't apologize," I assured her. "I get the same way. The reason I'm here in the first place is because I've already read through all the books I brought with me."

The way she smiled at that made my insides tighten. "It's always nice to meet a fellow book junkie."

I would have gladly stood there and listened to her talk until my arms got tired holding all those books. Unfortunately, the bell over the door chimed, alerting her to a new customer, so she left me to browse by myself while she got back to work.

I found another book I'd been meaning to read, as well as a couple more that looked interesting, then headed back to the register a few minutes later.

Holly had just finished checking out her other customer as I stepped up to the counter and set down my purchases to be rung up.

"Wow." Holly's friend, Naomi, came up beside me, propping her hip against the front of the checkout counter. "That's quite the haul you have there, hockey boy."

My brows rose up on my forehead. "Hockey boy?" I asked, humor laced through my voice.

She shrugged casually. "Don't know you well enough to get more creative just yet."

I could appreciate that. From what I remembered of the people I met the last time I was here, the town was full of quirky characters who only enhanced the charm of the town. Clearly, this woman rated high among them. "I can appreciate that. And as for the books, I'm a huge reader. These probably won't last me a month."

"Huh." She hummed thoughtfully. "What a coincidence. Our Holly here is also a huge reader."

I turned to the woman in question, my lips curving upward again. I couldn't remember the last time I'd smiled this damn much in such a short period of time.

Holly glanced up from the book she was ringing up and offered me another bashful smile as her cheeks pinkened once more.

"So she said." Under my attention, her blush rose higher on her cheekbones. "Which makes this the perfect place for me. I'm sure I'll be in here a lot while I'm in town."

"You hear that, Holls? He'll be in here a *lot*."

Holly cast her friend a threatening look before switching her attention back to me. "You're welcome any time. And I hope you enjoy these books. You'll have to let me know what you think."

"I have no doubt I will." I usually liked to get to know a woman a little better before I asked her on a date, but something about this one had my instincts screaming to act fast. She'd said that last part as a one-off, but I jumped on the opportunity it created. "I'd love to give you my thoughts, say, over dinner tomorrow night?"

Holly's lips parted and her eyes widened in shock, like she couldn't believe I was asking her out. I studied her features. Her delicate nose that turned upward ever so slightly, her perfect rosebud lips, and the rosy apples of her cheeks. I didn't see a hint of dishonesty in her eyes, which led me to believe this woman truly didn't realize what a knockout she was.

"Oh. Uh . . ." Holly seemed almost nervous, while I could practically feel the energy buzzing off her friend beside me.

"She'd love to!" Naomi chirped excitedly, earning herself a murderous glare from Holly that made my stomach drop to my feet. I didn't get turned down often, but it didn't take a genius to see that was the direction she was headed.

"Please ignore my friend. She has this condition where she speaks without thinking." She licked her lips and cleared her throat before continuing. "That's really sweet, but I'm afraid I have to decline."

I knew I failed at keeping the disappointment I suddenly felt off my face. "I'm so sorry. I didn't mean to make you uncomfortable. If you're seeing someone—"

"Oh, no. I'm single." And with those two words, the spark of hope came back to life. "It's just that I'm not really dating right now."

"Honey, don't be ridiculous," her friend Naomi butted in. "Of course you're dating," she declared before shifting her gaze to me. "Of course she's dating. And tomorrow is perfect."

"Naomi," Holly said in warning, but there wasn't a lot of heat behind it. Not that it mattered much to the tiny dynamo at my side. She didn't bother to glance at her friend as she tore a scrap of paper from the receipt machine and started scrawling something on it.

"Here. This is her number. Give her a call later to finalize the details. I promise, she's going to be so excited come tomorrow."

A part of me questioned if the tiny woman beside me was a little crazy, but another part of me really wanted Holly's number. There was no way in hell I'd force a date on her if she didn't want it, but at least this way, I could keep in contact without having to show up at her job day after day. And hopefully, after exchanging some texts, she'd warm up to the idea of a date.

Taking the slip of paper, I carefully folded it up and put it in my pocket. I gave Naomi a polite nod, but hit Holly with the most charming smile I could muster. "Ladies, it was nice meeting you both." Then I said specifically to Holly, "I really hope to see you again soon, Sunshine."

I managed to keep the victorious smirk off my face at her sharp intake of breath as I gathered up my things and headed back into the cold. I was going to have to give some real thought to how I was going to play this, because everything inside me was screaming to see that woman again.

Chapter Six

Holiday

I stood in front of the full-length mirror in the corner of my bedroom, examining the dress I was wearing and trying my hardest to keep my nerves at bay. Those bastards had been driving me crazy all day long, and I felt like I was going to spiral into a panic attack at any moment.

"I cannot believe I let you guys talk me into this," I said into the mirror, aiming my glare at my friends who were gathered in my tiny bedroom. When I bought this building for my bookstore, I was excited to find out there was an apartment upstairs. It wasn't the biggest space, and the fixtures and appliances were pretty dated, but there was no beating the commute. Plus, it was only me and my cat, Yoda, so I didn't need too much space.

However, with most of my friends crammed inside, I was starting to feel a little claustrophobic. Something that wasn't helping my nerves one bit.

My sister Sunny was sitting on the foot of my bed with her bestie and our recent sister-in-law, Blythe, both of them fishing through my jewelry dish for what they considered the perfect pieces. A very pregnant Rae was propped up against my headboard, eating the bowl of ice cream she had balanced on her belly as she okayed or vetoed the clothes Merritt and Ivy were pulling from my closet. Naomi was stretched across my bed beside her, lying on her stomach with her feet kicked up in the air.

She grinned unrepentantly at my reflection in the mirror. "Oh please. You're going to have the best time, and you know it. If you're mad at anything, it's that you know I'm right and you can't stand it."

I tugged at the high neckline of my dress, my top lip curling into a sneer. This absolutely wouldn't work. "I never should have let you talk me into going on this date," I grumbled. But the truth was, it wasn't Naomi's pushing that led me to agreeing to go out with the walking, talking sex on legs. We'd actually been texting a little since Naomi gave him my number without my permission, and he honestly seemed like a nice guy. He'd made me laugh and genuinely seemed excited to take me out.

The problem was, I didn't trust my own judgement when it came to men. Time had proven over and over that I was a shitty judge of character, and I couldn't help but question the instant draw I'd felt toward him when he walked into One More Chapter the day before.

"I should text him and cancel. Make up an excuse, like I came down with scarlet fever or something."

My room erupted with shouts of objection. Naomi knew me too damn well. She knew I'd probably chicken out of tonight, so she'd called in reinforcements in the form of pushy friends and sisters. With them here, there was no way they'd let me back out of this date.

The sound of my apartment door opening pulled me from the doubts swirling around in my head. "I'm here! I'm here." My friend and soon-to-be sister-in-law, Lennix, came rushing into my bedroom, making the space more cramped. "Sorry I'm late. Toby came home with a kitten he found in the barn by the lodge, and you know how that goes."

"Of course we do," I answered with a smile. "You're obsessed with all things furry." My bestie could never turn a blind eye to an animal in need and had a whole mess of rescue animals she'd saved over the years. I had no doubt that kitten was going to be the newest member of her menagerie. The only thing she was a bigger sucker for than animals was her and my brother Raylan's new foster son, Toby.

My big brother had started mentoring the boy shortly after he came to live at Hope House, a safe, thriving group home for foster children. Toby had lost his parents in a tragic accident, and my brother had bonded with the kid instantly. When Lennix came into the picture, she fell in love with him too. It was easy to do, seeing as he was one of the greatest kids on the planet. With the help of her parents, Lennix and Raylan made it through the process to become foster parents and didn't hesitate to move him into their home. It was only a matter of time before they adopted him and made it permanent.

"Nothing so far," Rae said around the spoonful of ice cream she'd just shoved into her mouth. "We're still trying to figure out what she should wear."

Lennix looked me up and down. Her face pinched up and she shook her head at what she saw. "Well, that dress sure as hell isn't it."

"What's wrong with it?" I asked, pinching the sides of the skirt and lifting them outward. I knew she was right, I just couldn't put my finger on *why*.

"You look like you're heading for jury duty and desperately want to make a good impression so they'll pick you."

Blythe snapped her fingers and pointed in my direction. "That's it! That's exactly what she looks like."

"Really?" Merritt stepped out of my closet to study me, her head canting to the side. "Because I thought she looked like one of those Mormons that go door to door trying to teach you about Jesus."

Everyone burst into laughter at her dead-on description. Even me.

"Did he say where he was taking you?" Ivy asked. "That would really help us decide what you should wear tonight."

I raised a shoulder in a helpless shrug. "He didn't say. And when I asked if I should wear something in particular, all he said was to dress comfortably. But I seriously doubt he meant sweats, or leggings and a baggy T-shirt." I threw my arms in the air and let myself fall back on my bed beside Rae's legs. I drew my hands over my face on a groan. "This is going to be a disaster. This guy is *way* out of my league. I never should have said yes." Though, as those words came spilling out, a tiny voice in my head screamed an objection. For as much as I complained, and as nervous as I was, there was also a part of me that was incredibly excited.

Tanner Fine was just that . . . *fine.* And the way he'd smiled at me yesterday in my bookstore had lit me up inside. Sure, I'd appreciated his good looks when he'd visited before, especially the way he wore that suit at Rae and Zach's wedding. I mean *dayum!* But that was from a distance, from the outside looking in. It was nothing compared to the up close and personal. Then when he smiled the way he did? It was game over. I wasn't sure there was a woman on the planet who would be immune to that.

"Hey, knock that off." Ivy grabbed my wrists and pulled them away from my face, using her hold to jerk me up to sitting. "First off, you are not out of *anyone's* league, you hear me?"

"Amen to that!" Lennix declared loudly while everyone else let out sounds of agreement.

"Second," Ivy continued, using her newly minted mom voice, "you have absolutely nothing to be nervous about. I know Tanner's this big deal in the hockey world, and the man has more money than God, but he's just a regular guy. He's down to earth and really sweet."

I gave her a flat look. "You say that now, but have you forgotten my track record with men? If he really is a sweet guy like you said, then whatever curse I have will most likely rub off on him and turn him into a prick, just like the rest of them."

"Oh, sweetie." Sunny scooted in next to me and wrapped an arm around my shoulder. "You aren't cursed, Holls. You've just picked shitty men in the past."

"Because my dick-head radar is broken."

She smiled pityingly. "No. Because you want to think the best of everyone. Even people who don't deserve it. It's not a bad thing . . ." She trailed off, squinting her eyes in thought. "Well, it's not *always* a bad thing. But you can't let past experiences jade you, or you'll miss out on something pretty great. That's not to say you shouldn't be cautious. Just don't say no to new experiences because you're scared."

"She's right, Holly," Lennix said. "Raylan kind of thought like you do, and because of that, he nearly messed everything up and lost the best thing that could ever happen to him," she said jokingly and waved a hand down her side to indicate herself, making me smile. She wasn't being conceited, she was speaking the truth. There was no woman on the face of the earth better for my brother than Lennix. "The fact that you don't see exactly how amazing you are in every single way makes me sad. You aren't out of anyone's league, they're all out of yours, and it's long past time you realize it."

"Did you not see how Tanner was staring at you the whole time he was in your shop yesterday?"

I would have been lying if I said that didn't perk me up just a little bit. "He was staring?"

She nodded enthusiastically. "Like a starving dog eyeing a T-bone steak. He barely looked my way, even when I was talking directly to him. Couldn't pull his eyes off you."

Rae picked up the conversation, rubbing my back comfortingly. "Not all men are like the ones from your past."

Sunny gave me a jostle. "Not all men are like the sperm donor who had a hand in creating us."

"Besides, you aren't looking for something serious, right?" Naomi reminded me. "You said you didn't want to date anyone, so look at tonight as what it is, the chance to have fun with a sexy hockey god who will hopefully show you a *fabulous* time." She waggled her eyebrows to really drive her innuendo home.

"She's not wrong," Lennix added. "I mean, a man that size has to be big everywhere, right? Unless he did something to seriously piss the gods off and they decided to punish him."

I couldn't imagine that was the case. Naomi's suggestion had sprouted roots in my brain and was growing like crazy. This didn't have to be a serious thing, and I was sure every woman in the country would give anything to trade places with me.

"Yeah. Yeah, you're right. This could just be . . . fun."

"Right?" Naomi patted my shoulder. "This could

just be a fun little fling. It's not like he's here to stay. He's just on vacation."

"But before any of that can happen, we *really* need to find you an outfit that doesn't look like it belongs on a 1950's housewife," Rae announced.

We got back to work, and thirty minutes later we'd collectively decided on something I felt stood firmly in the middle between casual and dressy. The fleece-lined leggings had a pattern up the sides that made them a tad fancier than the throw-around leggings I wore at home. I matched them with a pale pink sweater that draped off one shoulder and had a built-in camisole with lace straps. Instead of flats, I went with a pair of ankle boots that sported a chunky three-inch heel.

The pieces of jewelry Blythe and Sunny had picked out were delicate but understated, nothing overly flashy or chunky, and to finish it all off, I wore my hair down, having let it air dry into its natural waviness.

My girls all assured me that I looked perfect, and that tonight was going to be fun, and I tried my hardest to hold on to their excitement and not let my nerves run amok as they shuffled out of my apartment with less than five minutes to spare.

"What do you think, Yoda?" I asked my little buddy as he sat in the middle of my bed. "Do you think this works?"

He let out a series of short meows and mewls that sounded like he was trying his best to form words until the buzz of the intercom interrupted him. "Well, guess it's too late to do anything about it now, huh? Wish me luck." I leaned down to press a kiss to his head and gave him a little scratch beneath his chin that set off his purrs.

Then, with no other reason to delay, I pulled in a fortifying breath and headed for the door to buzz Tanner up.

Chapter Seven

Tanner

"Dude, you look like you're two seconds from hurling." Luke's voice carried through the speaker of my Range Rover as I drove through the winding streets of downtown Hope Valley. I was heading to pick Holly up for our date and I would have been lying if I said I wasn't feeling all kinds of nervous. Hell, I didn't even get nervous before games anymore, but that ray of sunshine, at least a foot shorter than me, had my stomach tangled in knots.

"Shut up, dick. I'm not gonna hurl." I didn't think.

My friend's grating laugh beat against my eardrums and set my teeth on edge. "I can't believe you asked a woman out. I thought you said you were taking a break after . . . what was her name?"

"Sandra, and I did. But there's something about this woman," I admitted. "I don't know what it is, but you should have seen me when I was in her store yesterday. I was following her around like a lost puppy."

"Damn, brother. That woman must have had game."

I couldn't help but smile as I recalled our interaction. "Actually, no. She was nervous and awkward. It was like she kept trying to melt into the wallpaper."

"Did she know who you are?"

"Yeah, but she didn't seem to care. I had to keep the conversation going just to keep her from walking away."

"Uh, buddy . . . are you sure this woman's interested?"

"Fuck off." I let out a chuckle. From the outside I could understand why it might seem like she wasn't interested, but I knew in my gut that wasn't the case.

"I'm just messing with you, man," Luke said, and I could hear the smile in his voice. "I'm happy you're getting out there again. Can't let a few bad experiences ruin everything."

I wouldn't consider what I'd dealt with in the past a *few bad experiences*. The number of opportunists was astounding. But I also knew it was what I was signing up for when I decided I wanted to be a hockey player. I was in the public eye, and my salary was plastered all over the internet. Gold diggers and users came with the territory. That was something I'd had to learn the hard way.

"Yeah, you're right. And this girl . . . I don't know how to explain it, man. There's just something about her."

"Sounds like you're really enjoying your time off. Glad for that, Tan. You needed a reset."

He was right. I needed this break. Some time away. I would have preferred it wouldn't have taken getting injured, but I could finally see the silver lining of the situation. The only thing putting a damper on this time away was the fact that I still didn't have a fucking clue what my future held. I was still dragging my feet on making the biggest decision of my life, much to my agent's dismay. But that was a problem for another time. "Anyway, I'm almost at her place, so I'll talk to you later."

"All right, brother. Don't forget to suit up. You know the rules, no glove, no love."

"Christ, you're an asshole," I said on a chuckle. "How you landed a ten like Lorna is beyond me."

"Brainwashing. But in all seriousness, enjoy yourself, man. You've earned it."

"Will do. Give Lorna and the kids my love. Talk soon."

I hit the button on my steering wheel, disconnecting

the call as I pulled up to One More Chapter. The sensation in my stomach reminded me of the way I felt every time I rode a roller coaster. Closing my eyes, I went through the series of breathing exercises I did every time I stood in front of my net. In a matter of seconds, I felt the familiar calm wash over me, and with a smile and a determined set to my chin, I killed the engine and climbed out of my car. It was time for another hit of sunshine.

I rounded the building like she'd instructed when we'd texted earlier, finding the buzzer panel beside the only door at the back of the building. I pushed the button and a second later, Holly's melodious voice carried through the speaker.

"Hello?"

"It's Tanner."

"Hi," she chirped, the sound of her voice making me smile. "Come on up."

At the buzz, I grabbed the knob and pulled the door open. There was a stairwell directly in front of me and against the wall to my right, and a short hall on the left that must have led into the bookstore from the back.

I had to make a conscious effort to go slow and not rush up the steps two at a time. Blowing a breath through pursed lips, I lifted my hand and knocked, and the instant the door opened, I nearly swallowed my tongue.

"Wow." It was the only thing I could say, because I couldn't think of a word to accurately describe how beautiful she truly was. "You look . . . just, *wow*."

That flush returned to her cheeks, and the sight of it was enough my make my dick twitch behind my fly. But when she smiled at me, there was no stopping the damn thing from going fully hard. I had about as much control over the thing as I did back when I'd been a teenager scoping out my first nudie mag.

"Thank you," she said in a low, genuine voice. "You look really nice too. I mean, more than nice. You look handsome." She clamped her mouth shut, her nostrils flaring with a deep inhale. "You look very wow too."

Christ, she was really something else, and it was taking everything I had to keep from kissing her right then and there.

HOLIDAY

. . .

I COULDN'T SEEM to stop making a fool of myself where this man was concerned, but just looking at him left me frazzled and nervous. He was just So. Damn. Sexy! And the megawatt smile he was wearing just then sent a shiver through my entire body.

Handsome didn't even cover it. The man quite literally made my heart skip a beat. I thought I knew what tall was, growing up with brothers that towered over me, but even they had nothing on the six-and-a-half-foot goalie. And it wasn't only his height that was impressive. He was just so *big*. The power in a frame like his should have been intimidating, and honestly, maybe even a little scary. But something in his eyes put me at ease.

I might not have been the best judge of character, but I couldn't imagine a man hiding a shitty side would have such warm, kind eyes.

Staring into Tanner's smile, a lightbulb flicked on inside my brain for the first time, and I quickly realized Blane's eyes never held that kind of reassurance, and maybe I'd been purposely ignoring signs that had been there from the very beginning. Maybe Sunny was right, and I'd only wanted to see the best in the men from my past instead of what was right in front of me.

The sharpness of his cheekbones, his prominent square jaw, and a masculine nose that had clearly been broken and reset—more than once, if I had to guess—

should only have added to his formidable presence. I was willing to bet the men he faced on the ice pissed themselves, but the only vibes I felt from him were soothing.

"And who's this little guy?" Tanner's deep, rich voice broke through my rapid-fire thoughts, and when I blinked back into reality, he was crouched at my feet, one large finger scratching Yoda beneath his chin.

That was all it took to make my little man fall in love. Yoda was more like a dog than a cat, willing to give his loyalty and affection for life just for some pets.

I bent and scooped the cat into my arms, rising to my full height so Tanner didn't have to remain crouched down. "Oh, this is Yoda. He's my little man."

The cat purred like the engine of a Harley as he received pets from both of us at the same time. "Wow, he's really sweet for a cat."

I lifted a beaming smile to Tanner. "I know. That's why I got him. It's the breed. They're known for being really affectionate."

To prove my point, Yoda let out his quiet little mewl, like he was trying to communicate, making Tanner laugh. "Okay, he's really cute. And the name fits him perfectly."

"Thanks. And I agree." I gave Yoda one last squeeze before putting him back on his own feet so he could head back into my apartment.

I pulled the door shut behind me, taking a moment to lock it even though you couldn't get into the building without the digital combination on the front and back exterior doors. "You think he'll be okay by himself for a while?" Tanner asked, his brow tugged together with concern as he stared at the door I'd just shut.

"Oh, he'll be fine. He'll curl up on one of the pillows on my bed and be asleep in no time."

He returned that deep amber gaze to me, making my insides melt a little. "If you say he's good, I trust you. So . . . you ready?" he asked, extending his hand to me.

Butterflies took flight in my stomach, but I pushed the sensation away and placed my palm against his, letting him wrap his massive hand around mine. "I am."

Sure, I still felt like I was out of my depth here, but seeing how he was with my cat worked wonders in untangling my frayed nerves a bit. I always believed a good indication of a person's character was how they treated animals. Blane, for instance, couldn't have been bothered to show Yoda an ounce of attention the few times he was around him. More often than not, he'd request I stay the night at his place instead of coming over to mine because he couldn't stand my "cat's constant need for attention". I should have dumped his ass right then and there.

Walking down my steps and out of the building

hand-in-hand with Tanner Fine was surreal. Not because he was a famous athlete, but because I couldn't remember the last time I'd held hands with a man like this. Despite the casual way he'd gone about doing it, there was an intimacy in the act itself, and warmth bloomed inside my chest as he led me around the building toward the street.

"It gets quiet pretty early around here, huh?" he asked as we closed in on the expensive SUV parked in front of my bookstore.

The sun was almost finished with its decent behind the mountains, painting the sky in smudges of dark blues and deep purples. "On this block, but it's not like we turn into a ghost town once the sun goes down. The Tap Room isn't far from here, and there are a few restaurants nearby that stay open late. That's where the crowds will be."

"That's good to know for the future." He pressed his thumb to the passenger door handle and the car beeped as the locks disengaged.

He pulled the door open and placed his hand on the small of my back to help me up. As soon as he closed the door, I pulled in a huge breath. The interior of the car smelled just like him. Like laundry right out of the dryer, or how it smells outside after it rains. It was fresh and clean and completely intoxicating.

"I hope you're hungry," he said as he climbed behind the wheel and pulled his seatbelt on.

My stomach chose that very moment to let out a very loud rumble. "I think it's safe to say I am. Now that the date has finally arrived, will you tell me where we're going?"

Bracing his forearm on the steering wheel, he twisted in his seat to face me, and I could have sworn he looked a bit uncertain. "I remembered how you said the days could get long for you, running the bookstore and everything. I figured that maybe you'd prefer to have a nice, relaxing night, so I thought I'd take you back to the place I'm renting and cook for you." His lips stretched into a wince. "But thinking about it now, and the fact that you hardly know me, I can see that might not have been the best idea; you might want something more public. At least until you're comfortable with me."

A pang of something hot and exhilarating ricochetted through me, reminding me it had been a *really* long time since I'd felt drawn to a man in any sort of way besides platonic. Not only did he remember I'd mentioned how work could tire me out, but he'd actually prepared for it, wanting to ensure I was able to fully enjoy myself. I couldn't remember the last time anyone besides my siblings or closest friends had taken my comfort into consideration.

"Tanner, that's incredibly thoughtful, and really sweet." I reached across the center console, placing my hand on his arm and giving it a reassuring squeeze. "And actually, a night in sounds perfect. Given you can actually cook and won't give me food poisoning or anything," I tacked on with an arched brow. After those text conversations, I'd started to realize he was pretty easy to talk to, and the longer I spent in his company the more that point was driven home. My nerves were slowly melting away.

He hit me with a megawatt grin, knocking the air right out of my lungs. "Don't worry, Sunshine. I know my way around a kitchen."

Why the hell was hearing him say that so damn sexy?

Chapter Eight

Holiday

The drive to his rental cabin had been surprisingly comfortable. No awkward silences or tension thickening the air. The more time I spent with Tanner, the more I realized what Ivy said was true. He might be a celebrity in a lot of circles, and he might have more money than I'd know what to do with in a lifetime—or so I heard; I refused to google him before the date, worried it would only stress me out more—but he was a normal guy.

A sexy mountain of a man rippling with strength and muscle, but still a normal guy.

Who just so happened to be renting the most beautiful house I had ever seen.

I sucked in a gasp of awe when we first pulled up

and I got a look at where he was staying. The word *cabin* was misleading. The place was more like a rustic mountain mansion made of wood, stone, and glass than it was a cabin. The inside was even more spectacular, with its incredible views of the foothills and forest. It was beautiful, and it was giving me some serious house envy.

Tanner had given me a short tour of the main living spaces, but before we could get more in-depth, my stomach let out another horrifying growl, so he insisted on starting dinner.

Now I was sitting at the oversized island with a glass of red wine he poured for me, watching him work.

He hadn't been lying about knowing his way around a kitchen. As I sipped my delicious wine in the dream of a kitchen, it was clear to see that, if anything, he'd down-played his skills.

He hadn't technically started cooking yet, but I could tell he was good simply by the way he moved around, pulling out ingredients and utensils with a level of comfort as only someone who knew what they were doing could.

"Are you sure I can't help with anything?" I asked again.

Tanner leaned back so he could see me around the opened refrigerator door. "Absolutely not." He pointed a finger at me. "You sit right there and relax. That's your only job this evening. I've got this covered."

I couldn't remember the last time a man had cooked for me, so who was I to argue? Lifting my glass, I took another sip. The wine was smooth and rich, probably the best I'd ever had, and from the vibrant flavors alone, I was pretty sure there was no way in hell I'd be able to afford a bottle myself, so I was happy to indulge while I had the chance. There was also the added benefit that it helped me feel warm and loose and not too nervous anymore.

I'd sent a pin to my girls with my location as soon as we got to Tanner's cabin, but the better I got to know him, the more certain I felt I was totally safe with him.

"Okay," Tanner started again from behind the fridge door. "I wasn't sure if you had any food allergies, so I got a couple options at the store earlier today." That melty sensation in my belly grew more intense at the realization that Tanner had actually gone grocery shopping himself in preparation for our date. "Lady's choice. I have everything for shrimp scampi over homemade pasta, but in case you can't eat shellfish or gluten I also picked up ingredients for chicken stir fry."

My god, this man was potent.

"*Homemade* pasta?" It would have been an impossible choice for me to make if not for those two words. I was a sucker for carbs in any and all forms, but pasta was my absolute favorite. And knowing he could make it by hand might as well have been my kryptonite.

Tanner's straight white teeth flashed in a smile he aimed in my direction before he lifted his bottle of beer and sipped. The man had the best smile. "Yep. And I take it by that look on your face that's the choice you're making?"

"Pasta is life," I declared with the proper seriousness a statement like that deserved.

Tanner's rough chuckle filled the space, warming the air around me. "Noted. Shrimp and pasta it is."

At some point, Tanner had folded the sleeves of his shirt, giving off some serious arm porn, and I was mesmerized by the way the veins in his forearms bulged and his tendons flexed as he got to work. Every single inch of him looked like it could be carved from stone and deserved to be displayed in a museum. And right at that very moment, he was cooking dinner for *me*.

"Okay, I'll ask one more time. Are you sure I can't help? I mean, making your own pasta is an impressive trick, but I can only imagine a dinner like this is a pretty involved process."

He shook his head, sending a lock of dark brown hair into his eyes before he lifted his arm to brush it aside with the back of his wrist. "You know, it's not really as hard as people might think. It's only flour and eggs. I'll start on the shrimp first, and while that's cooking, I'll get the pasta ready."

Well, if he was sure. Who was I to argue with the man when, instead, I could sit back and enjoy the show. A show entitled *Every Woman's Ultimate Fantasy*.

The pan he'd been heating on a low flame on the stovetop hissed as he dropped a few pats of butter into it. Then he got to work mincing garlic, his knife skills were like something I'd only seen on those reality television cooking shows. Watching him was as entertaining as all those professional chefs vying for the trophy . . . or cash prize, or whatever it was they won. I was so enraptured that his voice caused me to jolt when he broke the silence to ask, "So you own One More Chapter?"

I felt my face light up at the mention of my pride and joy. "I do, yeah. I opened it about four years ago."

Using the flat of his knife, he dumped the perfectly minced garlic in with the butter before turning his amber gaze on me with a tender smile. "And is owning a bookstore what you always wanted to do?"

I took a sip of my wine and lifted a shoulder in a shrug. "It took me a while to figure it out. I've been obsessed with books since I was a little girl. I always knew I wanted to do something involving them, I just wasn't sure how to make it a career. Having to learn proper comma placement insured that becoming an editor was out of the question, and even though I love stories, I never felt the pull to create any of my own. I'm perfectly content to leave that job to the professionals."

"So a bookstore it was."

"Exactly," I said with a soft smile of my own. "As soon as the idea hit, I couldn't imagine doing anything else. One More Chapter is my dream. It took a lot of time, a lot of trial and error, and a lot of blood, sweat, and tears—literally—but it's finally exactly how I've always wanted it to be."

The kitchen started to fill with the most delicious fragrances as Tanner seasoned the shrimp and added them to the pan with everything else. "You created something really magical, Sunshine." That was the third time he'd called me sunshine, and each time made my stomach swoop in the most pleasant way.

He got to work making the pasta. I'd seen it done before in Instagram reels, but witnessing the process in person was something else. Watching Tanner's large, strong hands form and roll the dough was downright erotic, and as the seconds ticked by, Naomi's suggestion to have a quick, fun fling was starting to sound brilliant.

"Thank you," I said, his compliment making the contents of my chest flip. I would never get tired of hearing people talk about their love for my store. "What about you? Did you always know you wanted to be a hockey player?"

Something moved over his features just then. The light in his eyes dimmed and the humor faded away from his expression.

"I'm sorry," I quickly stated. "You don't have to tell me. If I said anything wrong or overstepped—"

"No, it's fine." He shook off whatever thought had cast a cloud over him and curled a corner of his mouth upward. "I've always loved hockey. My mom used to joke that I learned to skate before I learned to walk." His features softened as he continued to talk about his years in youth hockey. As he went on to tell me about playing in high school and college, I felt a familiar bond forming between us. He was as passionate about playing hockey as I was about my shop, and seeing that in him as he spoke only made him that much sexier. Something I hadn't thought was even possible.

I wasn't sure how much more I could take. He'd already managed to knock this date out of the park, making it the best first date I'd ever had simply by paying attention and being thoughtful in his planning of it. Add in the cooking and the enthusiasm he wasn't afraid to show for his career, and I was dangerously close to melting into a puddle on the floor of this insanely gorgeous kitchen.

"I couldn't imagine doing anything else, and I consider the guys I play with my brothers. But there are downsides to it, like with anything."

Curiosity had me leaned in closer. "Oh?"

"Yeah, it can be incredibly hard on your body. I mean, that's why I'm here right now instead of finishing out the rest of the season. An injury took me out."

My face fell. "I'm so sorry. Are you okay?"

He waved away my concern. "It's all good now. Well, at least that part is. But I still wake up feeling like a seventy-year-old with arthritis, and my joints crackle like pop rocks in soda."

My eyes went wide and I slapped my hand over my mouth to try and catch the rest of my laugh that accidentally burst free. "I'm sorry," I croaked, fighting the tremble in my lips. "I didn't mean to laugh."

He joined me with a chuckle. "No, I get it. Trust me. Most mornings I'm awake at least five minutes before I'm able to climb out of bed."

And just like that, I was thinking about Tanner Fine in bed. Images of him dressed in nothing but boxer briefs as he slid out from beneath warm, silky sheets and stretched his long limbs played through my head in slow motion like that scene in *Fast Times* when Phoebe Cates climbed out of the pool. I pushed my wine glass away, knowing if I had much more the few inhibitions I still had would be gone in no time.

Along with my bra.

The conversation continued to flow with surprising ease as he finished cooking our meal and we finally sat down to eat. I laughed more through dinner than I had in a really long time. In fact, as I thought back, I realized I'd never laughed with Blane during our entire relationship as much as I had in a few short hours with a man I'd only just met.

"Oh my god," I moaned around my final bite. I placed my fork on my empty plate and pushed it away before I could do something embarrassing, like lick the damn thing clean. "Tanner, that was incredible."

I lifted my gaze to meet his, and my breath caught in my lungs at the heat in his eyes. He stared at my mouth like he wanted to devour something other than food. "Really glad you liked it, Sunshine." His voice was rougher, like he'd gargled with gravel.

I licked my lips and pulled in a shaky breath. "Like? Oh, I more than liked it. That was restaurant-level impressive." I managed to say, forcing the words past my Sahara-like throat.

Tanner sat back, twisting in his seat to better face me. There was something incredibly intoxicating about being the center of his focus. My skin prickled as heat built low in my core. "I can't believe I didn't notice you at that wedding," he said in that deep timbre that caused a shiver to course through me. It almost sounded as if he wanted to kick himself for missing me that night.

My brows rose to my hairline. "Given the fact you were there as my friend's date, I think it's a good thing you didn't," I teased.

His smile stretched a bit wider. "Of course. But I think it's clear Ivy and I were only meant the be friends from the very beginning. I ran into her, her husband, and their cute little girl the same morning I met you. They couldn't have possibly looked happier"

"Yeah, they are," I agreed, my heart giving a happy little squeeze for Ivy and her beautiful family. There was no chance Ivy would have been half as happy with anyone else as she was with Connor. "If I'm being honest, I kind of kept my distance from you that night. You were just so"—I waved my hand up and down, indicating all of him—"*you*. And in a suit too. I was way too shy to approach you."

The cocky smile he wore made him even sexier. "So what you're saying is you think I'm hot."

That flirty, teasing vibe he was giving off was infectious, and I couldn't help but flirt back. "I think you know you're hot."

He leaned in close and crooked his finger for me to

do the same. "I know something else too," he said softly, like he was sharing a secret.

"Yeah, what's that?"

The playfulness faded from his eyes, his expression growing earnest. When he spoke next, his voice was low and gritty, like his throat had been rubbed with sandpaper, and it dripped with the promise of something I didn't want to ignore. "I know that if I don't kiss you soon, I'm going to lose my mind, because I've spent all night desperate to know what you taste like."

I swallowed, my entire body erupting with tingles at his confession. "Tanner," I breathed, my heart threatening to beat out of my chest.

He lifted a hand, tucking a strand of hair behind my ear before trailing the pad of his finger down across my jawline. "Yeah, Sunshine?"

"Kiss me."

He did not need to be told twice.

Chapter Nine

Tanner

I couldn't have stopped myself if I wanted to. Not that I did. The woman had been tempting me all damn night simply by existing. She was funny and smart and had the biggest heart. It showed in how she talked about her family and friends. When she cared, she cared big, and that made her even sexier. How I'd managed to wait this long without kissing her proved I was even stronger than I thought. Until the very moment she gave me the green light.

With her requested kiss, I snapped. The instant my mouth crashed down on hers, I knew I was done for. A deep, needy groan ripped from my throat. My tongue came out, running across her bottom lip, and as soon as her mouth opened, I dove in.

She tasted like sunshine and sin. Like strawberries covered in rich dark chocolate. My hands came up to tangle in her silky hair, and damn if it didn't feel even softer than I'd imagined. I tangled my fingers deep, using my grip to tip her head back farther so I could take the kiss deeper. The little whimpers coming from her made me hard enough to pound nails, and when she fisted my shirt in her delicate hands to pull me closer, it took everything in me not to lay her out on the table so I could have my way with her.

As badly as I wanted to drown in this woman, I wasn't sure how much longer I could keep from ripping her clothes off. "Mmm, sweetheart." I forced myself to end the kiss, both of us breathing heavily as I pressed my forehead against hers. "We have to slow down or I'm going to lose my mind."

She chased after my lips, her eyes glassy with lust. "Me too."

I cupped her cheeks to keep her in place. "I don't want to take this too fast."

Holly nodded and tried pulling me in again. "Fast. Good. Let's go fast."

"No, baby, just listen." I grabbed her wrists and pulled them away so I could straighten up. I attempted a deep, calming breath, hoping it would get my throbbing dick under control, but all that did was fill my lungs with her citrus and spice scent. "I don't want to scare you off by moving faster than you're comfortable with." The only thing I wanted more than to be buried deep inside of her at that very moment was to know I'd get to see her again. I couldn't risk running her off because I moved too quickly.

"Tanner?"

I blinked, managing to clear a bit of the lustful fog from my brain. "Yeah, Sunshine?"

"Screw slow."

A sound like a record scratch blasted between my ears. "What?"

Her gaze was more focused than it had been a second ago. "I don't want to go slow, and you're absolutely not going to scare me off. I promise." She grabbed me by the face, squishing my cheeks together as she declared, "Believe me when I tell you I want this."

All rational thought flew right out the window in that instant, and I lunged. She let out a yelp when my hands spanned her waist and I hauled her out of her chair and into my lap. Our lips clashed together, and the only thought flying through my brain was that I would gladly drown in this woman.

HOLIDAY

I WAS HAVING an out of body experience. That was the only reason I could think of for why I was doing something so out of character. I wasn't against one-night stands. I'd just never had one.

Until tonight . . . hopefully.

I moved instinctively, spreading my legs wide on either side of Tanner's hips so I could settle more deeply on his lap. I swallowed down his groan and fisted his hair in my hands as my tongue came out and swiped across his lower lip. There might as well have been a gunshot starting off a race, because something in the mountain of a man I was currently straddling snapped.

If I thought he'd been wild before, it was nothing compared to the way he gripped my ass in both of his large hands. His fingers squeezed my flesh as he used his hold to rock the most sensitive part of me against the long, thick, steel rod I felt behind his fly.

A gasp ripped from my throat at the feel of him

pressing against me. Desperation and adrenaline coursed through my veins in place of my blood. That first kiss had rocked my freaking world. It had been the best kiss I'd ever had, and I knew, as his lips worked against mine and his tongue skillfully brushed my own, a man who could kiss like that could do so much more.

It was in that very moment I realized that every sexual experience of my life so far had been incredibly . . . *boring*. That had to be the case, because that first kiss with Tanner Fine was, hands down, the most erotic, thrilling thing I'd ever felt.

And I wanted more.

I wanted wild and passionate and exhilarating. I wanted to wash all that boring away, and my gut told me this man was more than up to the task.

A needy whimper slipped past my lips as Tanner continued rocking me against his erection, each brush causing my panties to grow wetter.

"Tanner," I panted when the need for oxygen forced me to break the kiss. I was pleading for something. I just didn't know what. But he didn't let up for a second. With my mouth free, he took the opportunity to drag his lips down the column of my throat, sparking to life erogenous zones I hadn't realized existed. "Oh my god. This feels so good."

I could feel my release building. My entire body felt

like it was about to go up in flames at any moment. But I needed *more.*

"Tanner," I said again, begging for something unknown.

"I know, Sunshine," he growled against my skin. "I know exactly what you need." I didn't have a doubt in the world about that, and I was totally willing to sit back —or lie back—and follow his lead. For a man I'd only started getting to know, I trusted him with this . . . for whatever reason.

My heartrate escalated and my breath stuttered as he pulled my hips tighter against his. "Tell me, Sunshine, are you wet for me?"

I sucked in a breath as I tried to focus on his face. It was harder than usual to do, given that I felt drunk on him. My tongue came out to swipe over my swollen, kiss-bruised lips. I opened my mouth to tell him yes, but I couldn't get my voice to work around the wad of cotton suddenly thick in my throat.

Tanner pulled back, his deep eyes lit with fire as they skittered across every inch of my face. His thick, expressive brows pulled into a frown. "Was that too much? Do you not like me talking like that?"

I'd never really given it much thought. I'd read plenty of it in books over the years, but fiction had been a far stretch from reality, at least in my case. Blane barely did more than grunt until he got off with a noise that was more akin to an animal being torn to pieces in the middle of the night by something much bigger.

But the way my body reacted to his words, the way my core pulsed as I grew even wetter, was all the answer I needed.

"No. I mean yes! Yes, I liked it. I'm just . . . I'm not used to it. But"—a smile pulled at my lips—"I really liked it."

His mouth curled into a deliciously wicked grin that made my insides feel like lava. "Good. Now answer the question. Are you wet for me right now?"

My chest rose on a jumpy inhale. "Yes," I finally admitted on a gust of breath. "I am."

He pushed his chair a few inches back and grabbed me by my waist, lifting me off his lap and onto my feet directly in front of him, cradled in the gap between his widely spread thighs. My heart was racing; it felt like something was crawling beneath my skin.

Tanner sat back in his chair, looking like the picture of casual relaxation as he braced an elbow on the arm of his chair and rested his chin in his hands. If not for the hard-on that looked like it was trying to burst through his zipper, I might have thought he was unaffected. His gaze was like a physical touch as it raked over me from head to toe, causing shivers to erupt across my entire body. "Then show me."

"What?"

"I want to see how wet I've made you. Show me. Take off your pants."

If it had been Blane giving that order, it would have given me the major ick, but those words coming from Tanner's mouth were molten. I was so hot I worried I would pass out.

Any other time, I might have been too shy, but something about him made me feel courageous, made me want to reach out and grab what I wanted. And what I wanted most at that very moment was him.

With a newfound bravery I didn't know I was capable of, I kicked off my shoes, hooked my thumbs in my waistband, and slid my leggings down my thighs until they pooled at my feet. The hungry rumble that traveled up Tanner's throat at the sight of my frilly lavender panties was like a hit of dopamine. I wanted to hear it again and again.

"Sit back on the table and spread your legs," he ordered, and I was helpless to do anything but obey. I took half a step back and bumped into the very edge of the table. I gave myself a single moment to send up a plea to whoever was listening that the table would hold my weight, then hoisted myself up. The finished wood was cool against my overheated skin, making me shiver as I braced my palms on the table behind me and slowly spread my thighs.

I felt like I was coming out of my skin. Like if he didn't touch me at that very second, I was going to combust.

Tanner's eyes had grown darker, reminding me of melted chocolate, as he dragged his tongue across his lower lip before pulling it between his teeth and biting down. "A little wider, baby."

I did as requested, and I knew without having to see for myself that the evidence of my arousal was obvious, having darkened the material where I'd been dripping.

"Jesus, you smell like heaven." Tanner leaned forward, so close I could feel the whisper of his breath against my sensitive skin. He inhaled deeply, his eyes rolling backward before falling closed. "I've been dying to do this."

"Tanner," I whispered, my arms starting to quake. "Please."

"You need me to touch you, Holly?"

More than anything. "Yes, please. *Please.*"

He hummed, the sound lush and sinful. "Christ, you

sound so pretty when you beg like a good girl. You know what good girls get?" I clamped my bottom lip between my teeth and shook my head. "They get rewarded." With that, he hooked a finger in the gusset of my panties and moved the lace aside. Then he buried his face in my pussy and began devouring me.

Chapter Ten

Tanner

I was going to come without even touching my dick. The taste of Holly was the best ever, and one swipe of my tongue was enough to make me an addict. Her sweet, honeyed arousal coated my tongue, and I lapped it up, greedy for more.

"Oh, god, Tanner. *Yes*," Holly cried out as she began to writhe on the table. "So good," she panted. "You're so good at this." Her whole body shuddered when I chuckled against her damp folds, and her arms gave out, leaving her stretched out before me like the most delicious meal I'd ever seen.

I was desperate to make her come, to hear the sounds she made as I pushed her over the edge. I moved to her clit, circling the tight bundle of nerves with the tip of my tongue as I worked a single finger into her tight channel. Her walls immediately clamped down around my digit, the flutters telling me she was already close. Thank god, because I didn't know how much longer I could wait to have her.

"T-t-tanner." My name stuttered from her mouth as her arms stretched above her head to grab hold of the other end of the table. "I'm close. I'm so close."

"I know, baby. I can feel you." I managed to get a second finger inside her, knowing I needed to get her ready for me if I had any hope of sliding deep into her warm, slick pussy. As it was, she was gripping my fingers like a vise. I couldn't wait to feel her choke my cock as she came around me. "Give it to me, Sunshine. Let me see how beautiful you are when you explode for me."

On that order, I sealed my lips down around her clit and sucked deeply as I speared my fingers inside her, focusing on her G-spot. With one brush of my fingertips, she went off like fireworks on the Fourth of July.

The sound of her pleasured screams made my prick pulse and beads of pre-cum drip from the head. She came so hard her thighs clamped down around my head, keeping me in place as her body began to quake. I stayed with her through every single moment, until she was little more than a puddle on the dining room table.

I sat back when her legs finally released me, taking

her in as I wiped my mouth clean with the back of my hand. Her chest rose and fell as she forced air back into her lungs, meanwhile, my own breath sawed in and out of my lungs like I'd blocked a hundred pucks coming at me in rapid fire. And I needed more.

"Don't pass out on me now, sweetheart," I warned as I lifted her off the table, giving her no choice but to wrap her arms and legs around me and hold on tight. "I'm just getting started. I need you conscious for what comes next," I teased as I began moving through the house with her in my arms.

"I can walk," she said quickly, squirming half-heartedly.

"If that's the case, I didn't do my job."

She hit me with a megawatt smile that nearly had me stumbling over my own two feet. "I mean your injury. Is it safe for you to carry me around like this?"

I was sure my PT and the team doctor would have a fit if they saw what I was doing, but I couldn't find it in me to give a shit. I wanted to hold on to her. I wanted her as close to me as humanly possible, and as long as she was okay with it, I had no intention of stopping.

"This is nothing, baby. I promise, I'm good."

That seemed to be all she needed to hear, because a moment later she slammed her lips down on mine in a hungry kiss that I couldn't bring myself to break, even though I couldn't see where the hell I was going.

Holly giggled against my lips every time I bumped us into something, and the sound lit my blood on fire. She had an incredible laugh. Almost as mesmerizing as her smile.

Thankfully, I made it to the main bedroom with only minimal damage to a few of the decorative pieces that had been in our path, and as soon as we were close enough, I tossed her onto the bed, reveling in her laugh and the way she looked, all that sunny hair spread out on my sheets. She looked like every single fantasy come to life, like she belonged in my bed.

Before I could tell her to do so, she pushed up, sat, and removed her sweater, leaving her in nothing but those sexy-as-fuck panties and a matching bra sheer enough to see her hard nipples pointing through.

"Fuck." I let out a gust of air. "You're so beautiful."

Her cheeks heated, the blush carrying from her neck to her chest, turning her soft skin a sexy pink that drove me crazy.

Her eyes were like melted pools of honey. "So are you. But I want to see more. I want to see *you*."

A cocky smile tugged at my lips as I started undoing the buttons on my shirt, one at a time, at a teasing pace. I put a lot of hard work in when it came to my physique. I had to in order to make my body work for me in the way my job required. My abs weren't quite as chiseled as some of the other guys on my team, but only because I was a hell of a lot bigger, which made cutting harder. But I was still strong as hell, and it showed in every other muscle.

I knew Holly liked what she saw the moment I stripped my shirt off and tossed it aside by the way she licked her lips and how her eyelids lowered to half-mast as they scoured over every bit of bared skin.

"Like what you see, Sunshine?" I asked with a cocky smirk. I couldn't help myself. The lust and desire in Holly's gaze as she took me in made my chest swell with pride, and I actually stood a little taller.

"Yes," she said, licking her lips. "I like what I see *very much.*"

Damn it, but this woman was going to be the death of me.

The need in her eyes moments ago disappeared, giving way to panic as I shucked my jeans and boxer briefs. She looked like she was about to swallow her tongue or possibly run in the opposite direction as she gaped at my straining erection. I could practically read the thoughts rushing through her brain just then.

"Don't worry, sweetheart," I assured her as I wrapped my finger around the base of my cock and gave it a stroke. Pre-cum immediately beaded at the very tip, and the relief at that simple touch was almost enough to take me to my knees. I'd been *aching* for her for hours, and I finally had her where I wanted her. "I'll get you ready for me. I promise I won't do anything to hurt you."

I felt a sudden sharp squeeze in my chest at that declaration, like something deep inside me demanded those words to mean more than something sexual. But that couldn't be the case. Right? I mean, I'd only just met this woman. But the pull I'd felt for her was unlike anything I'd felt before. It was intense and inescapable. A constant pulsing sensation beneath my skin.

My cock continued to throb, my need for her literally dripping from me. "Do you trust me to make this good for you, Holly?"

It took a moment, but she finally forced her focus from my dick to my eyes. Her eyes were wide as she blinked, and I found myself waiting with bated breath for her answer. Like it meant something more.

"Yes," she finally breathed out, and my shoulders actually slumped with relief.

Placing my knee on the mattress, I wrapped my fingers in the sides of her panties and pulled them down her long, smooth legs. Then I made quick work of her bra, unclasping it and tossing it aside, adding it to the pile of our discarded clothes.

"Spread for me, baby. Let me see that perfect pussy."

She didn't hesitate, showing me the proof of her arousal was already coating her inner thighs. "Jesus," I grunted as I drew closer. "You really are perfect everywhere, aren't you?"

The flush returned and her lashes lowered in that bashful way that made my dick twitch. "I'm far from perfect, trust me."

"Sorry, baby. But on that one, we'll have to agree to disagree." I leaned to the side, reaching into the bedside drawer for a condom. Sitting back on my haunches, I ripped it open with my teeth and slid it on before moving over her, bracing one forearm on the bed beside her head as I grabbed my cock and guided it to her center. I could feel her heat through the latex, and the most insane thought filtered through my brain. Images flew through my head like a flip book of me sliding inside Holly with nothing between us. Just skin on skin. Some baser, caveman part of me wanted to see my cum dripping out of her.

I had to shove those images down before I did something incredibly stupid. I'd learned a long time ago how conniving and underhanded some people could be. They'd been hard, painful lessons, but I'd promised myself I would never forget them.

Although when it came to Holiday Bradbury, it was

like all rational thought flew out of my head. I wanted to mark her. I wanted everyone who saw her to know that she was mine. Hell, I might as well have beaten my chest and dragged her back to my cave.

I didn't know what made this woman so different.

"Tanner," she whispered, yanking me out of my head and back into the present where the most beautiful woman I'd ever seen was laid out naked beneath me. Her soft hand came up to caress my cheek, and my eyes slammed closed as I leaned deeper into her touch at the same time I nestled my hips between hers and pressed the crown of my cock against her entrance.

She sucked in a breath as I nudged deeper, holding it in. "No, baby. You need to breathe. Try to relax."

Holly pursed her lips and exhaled slowly, her body melting into the mattress and loosening enough for me to slide in deeper. We both sucked in sharp gasps at the sensation. Nothing had ever felt as good as sinking into Holly. She fit me like a glove, her pussy squeezing like she wanted to hold me inside her forever.

Holly's neck arched, her head pressing deeper into the pillows as she took even more of me, inch by inch until I was buried as deep as I could get. There was no other way to describe it; Holly's pussy was the closest thing to heaven on earth.

"Ah, fuck," I groaned, her heat driving me crazy.

"You feel so fucking good." I squeezed my eyes shut and breathed deeply as I silently willed myself not to come too soon.

"Tanner," she said in a pleading tone as she wrapped those sinful legs around my hips, "please, move."

"Hold on, baby. I want to give you time to adjust. I told you I wouldn't hurt you." Though holding myself back was fucking killing me. To the point *I* was the one in pain.

Holly's heels dug into my ass like she was trying to force me in even farther. "I'm fine," she insisted. "But if you don't move, I'm going to go crazy."

She was killing me. "I'm trying to be careful with you." Because I now knew, without a shadow of a doubt, I'd rather rip off my own limb than cause her any kind of pain.

She brought her hands up, sliding her fingers through my hair before scraping her nails gently across my scalp. "Please," she said on a whisper. "Don't be careful. I'm not made of glass." Her heels dug in harder. "You aren't going to hurt me. I want you to do what you like," she said, almost as if she could see inside my head and already knew my preferences in the bedroom.

Any hope I had of taking it slow was shattered with that handful of words. My hips pulled back without any input from my brain, and I slammed forward, relishing the way her cunt began to flutter around me.

"That what you want, Holly?" I gritted out as I drove in and out of her like a man possessed. "You want me to fuck you hard?"

Her back arched as she clawed at my back. "Yes. *God*, yes. Don't stop!"

"Does my good girl like to be fucked rough and dirty?"

My words seemed to spur her on. She tightened around me, her hips rising up to meet my own with every thrust. "Please, *please*," she continued to beg like she was afraid I'd stop at any moment. Like I could if I wanted to. Which I absolutely didn't. I *craved* her, and I never wanted this to end. "I'm so close." Her eyes widened like she couldn't believe it. "Tanner, I—" Her words cut off when she curled her lips between her teeth and bit down.

"Fuck yes, Sunshine. Give it to me. I want to feel you come all over my cock."

She went off a second later, every muscle in her body locking tight as she clamped around me like a fist. She came on an explosion, screaming my name. If I thought she was beautiful when she came on my tongue, it was nothing compared to how she looked as she drenched my cock. It was impossible to hold off, and I followed her a moment later, burying myself as deep as I could get and growling my release into the crook of her neck. That caveman part of me reared its head, and all I could think was how badly I wished my cum was coating her pussy in that very moment. As it was, she'd ruined me. That sex hadn't just been the best I'd ever had. It had been out of this goddamn world.

When I was finally able to lift my head, I gave myself a few seconds to take her in. Her skin was flushed and glistening with a fine sheen of sweat. Her plump lips were swollen from my kisses, and that sweet honey gaze was glazed over. But the most beautiful thing was the way her lips had curled up in a small, pleased grin, like she was exhausted but still couldn't keep the smile off her face.

"You're extraordinary," I stated, even though that word felt less than adequate to describe her perfection.

Her smile grew wider as a giggle pushed past her lips. "I could say the same thing about you." Just then, her mouth opened on a yawn. "Oh man. It's really late isn't it?"

I twisted my head to get a look at the alarm clock on the nightstand. "It is, yeah."

Her features shifted, an expression that looked a lot like disappointment taking over. "I should probably go home."

There wasn't a chance in hell I was letting her go. Hell, I wanted to keep her with me as long as possible. If I had my way, we'd never leave this bed.

Leaning down, I sealed our lips and swiped my tongue against hers before pulling back, reveling in the way she lifted her head to chase after me. "Stay," I said quietly.

She blinked. "What?"

"If you want to go home, I'll take you. But I want you to stay. I want you to fall asleep in this bed, curled up in my arms. Then I want to wake up in the middle of the night and fuck you all over again. Then I want to do it all over again when the sun comes up in the morning."

I let my confession sink in, but as I waited, my heart had lodged itself in my throat.

"I want to stay too," she finally confessed. "And I want you to do exactly what you just promised."

I was starting to think there wasn't anything I wouldn't give her if she wanted it.

Chapter Eleven

Tanner

The sun was halfway through its rise, the colors of the sky still pale. I'd been awake for at least an hour, and I was still in bed. I hadn't been able to pull myself out, not when I had Holly's lush, warm body pressed against me, her face soft and tranquil in her sleep.

Her golden hair was fanned out across my pillow, and it was impossible for me not to touch it. Time had gotten away from me as I twisted and wrapped the strands around my fingers over and over.

At one point, Holly let out a series of little noises, and I worried I'd woken her, but she just rolled over and snuggled deeper beneath the covers before pressing into me again. Her bare shoulder was too tempting, so I leaned closer to her to press a kiss to it and started tracing patterns across her silky skin. I was addicted to her, and I wasn't going to bother denying it. Though, it wasn't only her body; I was addicted to her. I mean, I'd never written poetry in my life, but I would have gladly penned sonnets to her pussy. I was addicted to *all* of her. Her laugh, her smile, her sense of humor and kindness. The sound of her voice and the way she lit up talking about her friends and family.

She was lying right beside me, skin to skin, but it didn't feel like enough. I still craved her, and my gut told me that desire wasn't going to lessen any time soon.

At that thought, my phone rang with an incoming FaceTime call. I quickly rolled over and silenced the call before it could wake Holly up. Not wanting to risk the person calling back, I carefully slid out of bed, as much as I didn't want to, and pulled on a pair of sweats before slipping silently out of the room with my phone.

As I expected, the ringing started again a few minutes later, just when I finished brewing a cup of coffee. I brought the steaming mug to my lips, rounded the island, and pulled out a stool. "I know your ass has to be up early, but did you forget I'm supposed to be on vacation?" I said instead of hello.

Luke's ugly mug grinned through my screen, and I would've given anything to be able to reach through the phone and punch him. "You're usually already up by now," he pointed out. "Even on vacation." He arched a brow. "Unless you have good reason for sleeping in. Say, didn't you have a date last night?"

"Shut the fuck up, man," I grumbled, but I couldn't stop the goofy smile from overtaking my face.

"Holy shit, dude! I was just messing with you. But did you really . . ." he trailed off and waggled his eyebrows like a fucking moron.

"I'm not talking to you about shit like that."

Luke's face pulled into a sarcastic pitying wince. "Oh, brother. I'm sorry. You weren't able to . . ." He made a gesture with his finger like it was a drooping dick.

"You're a prick," I said on a chuckle. "I mean I'm not talking to you about shit like that because it's none of your business."

"Fair enough. But don't think I missed that smile, man. You looked downright giddy."

I couldn't really argue with that, so I didn't bother trying. "The date went well."

Luke pointed through the screen at my face. "I figured that from the hickey on your neck there, buddy."

Ah, shit.

I lifted my free hand to slap it against the side of my neck, and the instant I did, Luke's eyes bugged out and he burst into laughter. "I was just fucking with you, but at least now I know the date went well."

I didn't bother hiding my smile. I didn't want to. "Yeah. It went well. She's . . ." I scrubbed a hand down my face as I tried to search for adequate words. "She's incredible. I don't know how else to describe her."

He studied my expression, his gaze shrewd. "I've never seen you like this, man."

"I've never felt like this," I admitted. "She's different, brother. I can't explain it. I just . . . *I* feel different when I'm around her. I've never felt like this about a woman before."

Luke was silent for a beat, like he needed a moment to take in everything I just confessed. "I'm happy for you, Tan. Honestly, I am. But I just want to make sure you're being smart. That you're looking out for yourself first and foremost."

I understood his concern. He'd been there for me when shit had gone down in the past. It was unbelievable what some people were capable of when money or fame was involved. I'd met more than my fair share of women who wanted nothing more than to use me for both those very things. Women who would go to ridiculous lengths just to catch me in a compromising position so they could profit off it.

"I get why you'd worry, but I'm not an idiot. I learned to look out for myself a long time ago."

Luke blew out a heavy sigh. "I know that all too well. Nothing would give me more pleasure than to punch your piece-of-shit father in the fucking face."

My mood began to dim, something I hadn't thought possible after the night I had. But that was what talk of my father always did. "He's not worth it."

Something over my shoulder caught Luke's attention, and a shit-eating smile. "Well, good morning," he said before his attention came back to me. "Now I *really* see how your date went well."

My back shot straight, and I looked over my shoulder to find Holly standing in the entryway of the kitchen. She was dressed in my button-down from the night before, her hair hanging loose and slightly disheveled from sleep, and in her just-waking-up rumpled state, she was more beautiful than I'd seen her so far.

"Hi," I said, once again struck mute by this incredible woman.

"Hi back. I didn't mean to interrupt." She pointed at the phone I was still holding, the screen facing her clear as day.

"You didn't," I assured her at the same time Luke spoke up. "He's right. I called him at the crack of dawn to give him a hard time since his lazy ass gets to be on vacation. If anyone interrupted, it's me."

She smiled at my best friend, her whole face lighting up. "That's okay. I'm sure Tanner can use you giving him a hard time now and then. Keeps his ego in check."

"Oh, I like her," he declared.

My lips hooked into a smirk as I eyed her up and down. "Yeah, I do too. That's why I'm hanging up on your ass." I didn't let him get a word out before I hit the button disconnecting the call. Placing my phone face down on the island, I swiveled on my stool to face her full-on as she walked farther into the kitchen. As soon as she was within reach, I snagged her by the wrist and yanked her between my legs. My free hand hooked behind her neck so I could pull her down for a slow, thorough kiss.

"Good morning," I said with a smile against her lips.

"I'll say." She pulled back and beamed down at me.

Now that she was in the room, the desire to touch her became a physical thing. My palms itched like there were bees under my skin. "I hope I didn't wake you up. I wanted to let you sleep." It was still early, the sun was still ascending, after all.

She shook her head, wrapping her arms around my neck and perching her full, round ass on my thigh. "No,

I'm used to getting up early so I can open the shop every day."

"Do you not have any other staff?"

"Oh, I do. I have three girls. They're amazing, and One More Chapter wouldn't be what it is today without them. It's hard for me to schedule them early in the morning. I feel too guilty."

I lifted my hand to brush a few wild strands of hair back from her forehead, then trailed my fingertips down her temple and over her jaw to cup the side of her delicate neck. Her kind heart was one of the things that made her so damn attractive. "Sounds to me like they're lucky to have you as a boss."

"Or maybe we're all lucky."

And there it was again. She really was something else.

Her mouth stretched open, her jaw cracking with a yawn. Once she was finished, she pointed at my mug. "Got any more of that?"

"Of course. Let me make you a cup." I shifted her off my lap and onto the stool in my place and set another cup to brew in the single use machine that came with the house.

"I heard what your friend said about protecting yourself," she started, catching me off guard.

I sputtered for a second before finally getting the

words out. "No, sweetheart, it's not what you think. He wasn't trying to offend anyone—"

"Oh, no. I get it. I wasn't offended. In fact, I'm glad you have a friend who looks out for you like that. I just want you to know that you don't have to worry about that with me."

My brows tugged down in a frown as I slid the mug to her across the island and headed for the fridge. "What do you mean?"

She took the creamer option I held in my right hand and doctored her mug as she continued. "I mean that I get it. I know what last night was, and I don't expect anything from you."

My chin jerked back. "What do you think last night was?"

At my tone, Holly's face pinched up in confusion. "What do *you* think last night was?"

One corner of my mouth curled up in a smirk. "Oh no, Sunshine. I want to hear your answer first."

Her expression grew stubborn. "I don't want to say."

I chuckled, giving my head a shake. "Fine. What I think last night was, or at least what I hope it was, is the start of something pretty fucking great."

Her lips began curving up slowly, her grin teasing into a smile until she was beaming with it. "Really?"

I couldn't stand the distance between us for another

second. Skirting the island, I took her by the hips and lifted her up, depositing her on the island and stepping in close. "Yeah, really." Her skin felt like silk beneath my palms as I slid them up and down her outer thighs. She spread them wider, making room for me to step between them. "I know we don't know each other very well yet, but I really like you, and I'd like to know you better. I want to spend more time with you. A lot more time, actually. If that's all right with you." I smiled wide at the sound of her giggle. "That's what last night was for me. But if it was something else for you, I understand. I'd never force you into something you don't want."

"I like you too," she confessed, and the band that had been constricting my lungs loosened, allowing me to take in a full breath. "And I'd like to get to know you better."

There was that small, niggling voice in the back of my head reminding me that my time in this town was temporary; I still had to make this huge decision about my future. But I shoved it into the deepest, darkest recesses, content to ignore it for the time being.

"Now that we've gotten that out of the way, how about I make you breakfast. Then I'll take you back upstairs so I can give you the rest of the tour. The shower in the primary bathroom is out of this world."

Her brows winged up toward her hairline, and she let out a bubble of musical laughter that lit me up inside.

Chapter Twelve

Holiday

Tanner hadn't been lying about the shower. In fact, the whole bathroom looked like it belonged in an interior decorating catalogue. The stone counters were a creamy white with veins of grey. The tile floors were heated, as were the towel racks. It was heaven in the form of a bathroom, and any other time I would have been drooling over it. But there was something else that stole my attention and had me drooling.

The bathroom was filling with steam and the scent of freesias.

"Are floral essential oils good for sore muscles or something?" I asked teasingly as Tanner stepped back from the shower and screwed the cap back onto the bottle.

"Smartass," he returned, a smirk playing on his sexy mouth that made my stomach feel warm and floaty. I felt like I'd walked on air since the night before, and everything Tanner said and did only made that sensation linger. I kept pinching myself, waiting to wake up, because this had to be a fairy tale. It couldn't be real life.

"I'll have you know, these were part of the welcome basket the owners left for me when I arrived." He lifted the bottle and sniffed. "But I'm comfortable enough in my masculinity to admit this shit smells amazing."

My head dropped back laughing, and when I brought it up again, Tanner was standing right in front of me. "God, you're beautiful when you laugh," he said in a reverent tone, reaching up to tuck a lock of hair behind my ear. My skin broke out in goosebumps as the pads of his fingers skated down the side of my face. His thumb brushed back and forth against my lower lip, setting my body aflame all over again. "Hell, you're beautiful all the time."

God, my skin felt like it was in a constant state of blush around this man! Butterflies took flight in my belly as heat pooled in my core. A shy smile curled the corners of my lips as I looked at him through the fan of my lashes.

"Oh, believe me, there are times when I'm far from beautiful." Like on the first day of my period when I was bloated as hell, moody, and couldn't find the energy to brush my hair or teeth. On those days, I usually wore my rattiest sweats, the ones I'd stolen from one of my brothers at some point. They were stained and faded and full of holes, but they were also soft as clouds, and all I gave a damn about on those days was comfort.

He shook his head like he couldn't believe it. "Nah, I think I'd find you hot even if you'd rolled around in mud."

I arched a single brow. "Doubtful, but you're also not going to find out. I don't make a habit of rolling around in the mud."

He hummed in thought as he grabbed my hips and lifted me onto the bathroom vanity. I let out a squeak at the chill of the marble against my bare butt. He smiled as he continued to touch me, trailing his rough palms along the outside of my thighs. Up and down, up and down, in a slow, tantalizing rhythm that was quickly driving me out of my mind. "That's a shame," he murmured, the rasp in those words making it sound like his throat was coated with gravel.

"Oh?"

His smirk promised all kinds of things I wanted right

that moment. "Oh yeah. Because if you were that dirty, I'd get to take my time cleaning you up."

I brought my fingers up to toy with the button between my breasts. "Well," I started, giving him a teasing smile. "You could always *pretend* I'm dirty." I slipped the button from its hole, giving Tanner a better peek at my cleavage.

A rough growl tore from his throat just a moment before his mouth came crashing down on mine in a searing kiss that lit me up. His tongue brushed over my lower lip before he pulled it between his teeth and gave it a stinging nip. The pain of that fled instantly, leaving a molten pleasure in its wake as Tanner plundered my mouth.

I was wet for him in no time, my fingers clutching at the waistband of his joggers as I tried to pull him closer.

Tanner's fingers started on the buttons of the shirt I'd stolen again, but got frustrated halfway through. Gripping the lapels, he ripped the shirt open the rest of the way like a man possessed. I sucked in a surprised gasp as the humid, steamy air kissed my suddenly-exposed skin.

A hungry, primal sound rattled up Tanner's throat from deep within his chest as he separated the material, skating his fingers over my shoulders to push it off. I sat on the vanity in front of him, completely naked and at his mercy, yet I'd never felt more powerful. I could bring this mountain of a man to his knees with barely any effort, and knowing that was almost as intoxicating as the way his eyes suddenly darkened like the midnight sky and heated into molten pools.

"Christ, what you do to me," he muttered as his gaze swiped over every inch of me, like he was trying to commit my body to memory. My nipples pebbled into painfully hard peaks and my breathing grew short and choppy. My heart started beating faster. I felt like I'd just finished running wind sprints for an hour and he hadn't even really touched me yet.

"I might have an idea," I said quietly, my voice coming out short of breath. Because that was what he did to *me*.

"Look at you, Sunshine," he continued, his tone reverent. "I don't think I'll ever get tired of looking at you."

God, I was coming out of my skin. "I appreciate the sentiment, really, but if you don't touch me, I'm going to lose my ever-loving mind."

That was apparently the green light he needed. Cupping my left breast, he lifted it at the same time he bent lower, and tucked my nipple into his mouth. He drew hard, creating a throb that echoed all the way between my thighs.

I let out a sharp cry as pleasure melted me into the counter. I reached behind me and braced my hands on the counter to keep from falling into the mirror.

As Tanner continued to assault my nipples in the most perfect way, switching back and forth to give them equal treatment, I began to writhe, my core achingly empty and greedy for him.

"Tanner, please," I pleaded, not feeling a single ounce of shame. That had disappeared the night before. That dominant side of him brought something in me to life. I hadn't known what I was missing—what I needed—until he showed me. Owning my own business was a lesson in control. I was in charge day in and day out, and my night with Tanner taught me something. When it came to the bedroom, I didn't *want* to be in control. I wanted to be told what to do, taken care of. I wanted to be used for pleasure, then doted on like I was the most important thing in the world. "I need more."

As if he had to see for himself, he slid one hand between my thighs and cupped my pussy. His eyes rolled back on a groan as the wet heat at the apex of my thighs showed him just how needy I was.

"Does my good girl need something stuffed inside this pretty little pussy?"

My god, he turned me on to the point I thought I

might be able to come just like this. But that wasn't what I wanted.

"Yes. *Please.* I need you inside me."

"You mean like this?" My lips parted on a silent shout as I clenched down around the digit. It felt amazing, but it still wasn't enough. "Or do you need my cock?"

On a whimper, I curled my lips between my teeth and shook my head.

He traced beneath my bottom lip. "Need your words, baby. If you want me to fuck you, I need to hear you say it."

Reaching up, I took his face in my hands and pulled him closer. "Tanner. I need you to fuck me. Please, fuck me."

I barely got the last word out before he shoved his pants to the ground, scooped me off the counter, and carried me into the shower. The water was the perfect temperature as he twisted, taking a seat on the tile bench that stretched across the back wall of the massive space, never once breaking the kiss. Our tongues thrust against each other's in the same rhythm as my hips circling over his lap.

Tanner's fingers tangled in my wet hair at the back of my head, fisting the strands for better control. "Fuck, I can feel how hot you are," he grunted as his other hand came down to my hip, his fingers digging hard into my skin. "I want to watch you ride me. I want to feel your cunt squeeze the life out of my cock before you come all over it."

I couldn't wait another second. Lifting up on my knees, I reached down between us and held his thick, rigid cock straight so I could lower down on it. I moaned at the way he stretched me wider than any man in the past ever had. Taking him was a slow process, but the instant I was fully seated I began to rock, unable to hold back for another moment.

"Fucking heaven," Tanner gritted out against my lips as his fingers pressed hard into my hip and his grip on my hair tightened. "Pretty sure nothing on this planet feels as good as you."

"Oh god, Tanner," I whimpered as the pressure in my core began to build. I rocked harder, faster, circling my hips before lifting up and dropping back down, taking him fast and deep.

"That's right, Sunshine. Ride that cock. Fucking own it." His hand came down on my ass with a resounding crack that bounced off the warm tiles. The glass doors were completely fogged up, making it impossible to see out, but that was fine with me, since Tanner was the only thing that held my attention.

"It's so good," I panted. My tits bounced as I took

him rougher, feeling the head of him hit something deep inside me that was both painful and exquisite at the same time. "I'm close. I'm almost—"

"That's my good girl. Get there, Sunshine. Show me how fucking good my fat cock makes you feel."

His words were all it took to push me over the edge, and I screamed out my release until my throat felt like I'd swallowed sandpaper. Tanner's hips began lifting off the bench, driving deeper inside me, and a second later, he swelled impossibly thicker before following after me and roaring out a sound that set off a second climax in me.

I collapsed against him, wrapping my arms around his shoulders and burying my face in the crook of his neck as I came down from the most amazing orgasm of my life. "Oh my god," I said once I was able to breathe again. "That was so good. Why was it so damn good?"

Tanner looked down at his lap, his brow furrowing. "I think I might know why." He lifted his gaze to mine. "Holly, baby . . . I forgot to put on a condom."

Chapter Thirteen

Holiday

It took my brain a few seconds to catch up to what he'd just said, but that was enough time for Tanner to assume my silence was a freakout. "Sunshine, I'm so sorry. I wasn't thinking. I swear, this has never happened before."

"So you've never had sex without a condom before?" I asked, for clarification.

He shook his head, running his hand down the back of my hair. "Never. I'm clean, if you're worried about that. And besides that, I get regular physicals. If you want to see for yourself, I'm more than happy to show you."

I probably should have been freaking out, or at the very least concerned, but for some reason—maybe the earth-shattering sex and orgasms—I was fine. I believed him when he said he was clean, so instead of worrying about everything, I decided to just roll with things and enjoy this while it lasted. I'd felt more alive the past several hours than I had in a long time, and I wasn't ready to give that up.

"It's okay."

"I can't believe I—wait. Did you just say it's okay?"

I couldn't help but smile. He was really cute when he was flustered. "I did. Because it is. I'm clean too, and I have an IUD, so you don't have to worry about me getting pregnant either."

He frowned for some reason, but before I could ask why, my stomach let out a rumble, pulling him back into the present. He smiled, wiping water droplets off my face with his middle and index fingers. "I guess I didn't feed you enough at breakfast, huh?"

I lifted my shoulder in a shrug. "Well, you've given me quite the workout lately. More than I'm used to, that's for damn sure."

He chuckled, his smile unrepentant as he lifted me off his lap and placed me on my feet before standing from the bench. "Then let's get you cleaned up and reheat what's left from breakfast."

He insisted on washing my hair and scrubbing my body, his touch so tender it created a burn on my nose and the backs of my eyes. I had to blink to fight back the tears that wanted to fall. He was so damn sweet. Unless he was being dirty, but even that was better than I could have imagined.

Once we were both clean, we climbed out and Tanner wrapped me in a plush, oversized white towel. I dressed in my clothes from the day before and wrapped my damp hair into a bun on the top of my head before returning to the kitchen. That time around, Tanner was dressed in a pair of jeans and a long-sleeved thermal that hugged his muscles perfectly.

He turned his head at the sound of my footsteps and grinned over the rim of his coffee mug. "Hey gorgeous." He lifted the mug in his hand, asking, "Want another cup?"

"Yes, please," I answered immediately. I lived on caffeine at all hours of the day. As he worked on brewing a cup for me, I slid one of the stools out and took a seat. He must have reheated the breakfast he made earlier, because there was already a plate sitting on the island, and I didn't hesitate to dig right in.

The perfectly crisp bacon from earlier was now a little droopy, but it didn't affect the taste at all. I crunched into a piece. I hadn't been joking about Tanner giving me a workout. I'd probably burned more calories in the past twelve hours than I had in the last year.

A minute later Tanner slid a mug in my direction. I lifted it to my lips and drank, my eyes widening in surprise that he remembered how I'd taken it earlier. "Thank you for all of this. I think I can say with confidence that this is the best first date I've ever been on." Though it didn't feel like a first date. At least not anymore. All my usual hangups when it came to first dates were notably absent. It felt like I'd known Tanner for years, not less than a handful of days.

"Glad I could be of service." He bent forward, resting his forearms on the island across from me. His presence was as potent as ever, even with the large slab of marble between us. "But it was the least I could do."

I arched a single brow. "Yeah, well, it's more than someone besides my family has done for me in a really long time." And how sad was that? "I'm feeling a little spoiled over here," I confessed as I scooped up a bite of eggs and stuffed them into my mouth.

"Better get used to it, 'cause I plan to spoil you as much and as often as I can."

For a few more weeks, I thought to myself, the reminder dulling some of my shine. I shook my head to clear it of that unhappy thought and pushed it to the darkest, deepest recesses to dredge up later. For now, I was choosing to stick my head in the sand so I could enjoy it while it lasted.

I moved the food around on my plate as a thought I had been curious about since earlier that morning came to me. "Um, so . . . can I ask you a question?"

"Sure," he answered without hesitation before taking another drink of his coffee. "Anything you want to know, just ask."

I slicked my tongue across my bottom lip before biting down on it.

"Hey." he stretched his long arm across the island and placed his hand over mine to still the fork I'd been scraping over my plate. I hadn't realized I was still doing it. "You don't need to be nervous. I'm an open book."

I released my lip and smiled. "I was wondering about your dad." I didn't miss the way his muscles tensed up before he forced his body to relax. "I'm sorry if that subject is too personal. I overheard you and your friend." I realized how that sounded as soon as the words were out of my mouth. My eyes bugged out and I immediately tried to backpedal. "I wasn't trying to eavesdrop, I swear—"

"Holly, it's okay." His smile put me at ease instantly. "I know you weren't eavesdropping. I wasn't exactly keeping that call private."

"Okay." I let out a sigh. "It's just that I overheard you and your friend—"

"Luke."

"Right. Luke. He said something about wanting to punch your father in the face . . ."

Tanner pushed an audible exhale out of his nose as he rose to his full height. I had the impression he was trying to prepare for whatever he was about to say as he finished off the last of his coffee and deposited the empty mug in the sink. "My father," he said in a tone I hadn't heard from him yet. Hard and cold in a way that made me shiver.

I waited, cupping my mug with both hands as he moved toward me. He pulled out the stool beside me and sat down, scrubbing a hand over his face on a weary sigh.

"Hey, you don't have to talk about it if it's too hard."

"No, it's fine. Honestly. Truth is, I don't have much of a relationship with the man. Never have. He wasn't the kind of man who had any business having kids, really." I knew how true a statement like that could be, seeing as *neither* of my parents had any business having children. "He bailed on me and my mom when I was a kid. Just walked out of the house one day and never came back." He shook his head and massaged the bridge of his nose. "I remember how worried she'd been. Frantic, really. For days. She even called the police to file a missing person's report."

"Oh, Tanner." I reached out, my heart suddenly aching for him, and placed my hand on his arm.

"That was how we found out the truth," he said bitterly, shaking his head on a sardonic laugh.

"We had to find out from the cops who went searching for him that he wasn't lost or hurt, he was shacked up in some roadside motel with a hooker. My mom was scared to death that he was dead somewhere, when really he just didn't want to be a dad or a husband anymore."

My own parents were worthless wastes of oxygen, but at least they'd done us the courtesy of letting us know they weren't coming back. I couldn't imagine what his poor mom had suffered through.

"I wrote him off after that," Tanner continued. "Not that it really mattered. It wasn't like he was going out of his way to have a relationship with me. After that went down, life sort of moved on. It wasn't always easy. I mean, my mom had to work her ass off now that we were down to one income. And hockey is expensive as hell. We even had to sell the house we were living in and move into something smaller. But Mom," he paused, his features softening and a warm smile tugging at his lips, "she was a freaking rockstar. She knew how much hockey meant to me because she never missed a game or a practice, and despite the cost, she made it work."

"Tanner. That's incredible. She sounds like an amazing woman."

"She is," he said, pride lighting his expression. "I couldn't have asked for a better mother."

"Is she in D.C. with you?"

He shook his head. "No, she lives down in Florida with my step-father."

"I'm glad she was able to meet someone better."

"Yeah." He chuckled as he scratched the back of his neck. "Funnily enough, he was my high school hockey coach." I bugged my eyes out in shock, causing him to laugh harder. "Yep. It was really weird for me at first. Apparently he'd been crushing on her for years. He'd see her at all my games, all those booster meetings to raise money for the team. I'd always liked the guy, and I when I saw how he treated my mom, how he made her smile, I decided I wasn't going to stand in their way. She spent years working her ass off after my dad bailed, then Andrew came in and did everything in his power to make her life easier."

I propped my chin in my palm, offering a genuine smile. "He sounds pretty terrific."

"He is. And he's a great step-dad. When they decided they wanted to retire somewhere warmer, I moved them to Florida and bought my mom her dream house."

"You're a great kid," I said softly, that warmth blooming in my chest all over again.

"I am who I am because of her," he returned with a modest shrug. "And Andrew came into the picture just in time to teach me what it meant to be a man. A house and a membership to a country club so he could spend the rest of his days playing eighteen holes of golf is the very least I could do. Believe me."

"And your father—the biological one—he wasn't around for any of it?"

Tanner shook his head, some of the light fading from his eyes. "Nah. At least not until I made it into the NHL." My stomach plummeted, and I had a sneaking suspicion I knew what he was about to say. "As soon as that bastard found out I had money, he came crawling out of his hole. Suddenly he was this proud dad. Told anyone who would listen that he was Tanner Fine's old man."

"What a fucking dick."

Tanner's eyes shot up to mine, a bewildered laugh bubbling past his lips. "I don't think I've heard you cuss like that before."

I shrugged primly. "I have no problem with it when it's warranted."

"And you feel like it's warranted for my dad."

"I *know* it is," I specified. I considered myself some-what of a genius when it came to shitty parents. And from the sounds of it, Tanner Fine's biological father broke the mold.

"When I made it clear I wanted nothing to do with him, he started showing up at the stadium. He was drunk half the time and got off on making a scene. He'd go on and on about how ungrateful I was, how he'd gotten me to where I was today. And when that still didn't get a reaction out of me, he sold some bullshit story to a two-bit gossip columnist painting me as the bad guy."

Okay, now I wanted to hunt the jackass down and beat him senseless.

"What happened after that interview came out?"

His chest rose and fell on a deep breath. "Well, my agent and everyone told me not to respond, that it would go away with time. That was hard as hell, especially when people started talking shit online like they actually knew me. But I did my best to let it roll off like water off a duck's back. But then some asshole who thought himself a detective started digging into my mom. When stories about how I'd set her up in this cushy lifestyle and left my father to rot, I couldn't stay silent anymore."

"That couldn't have been easy, airing all your personal history like that for strangers."

"It might not have been if it hadn't been my mom's name in their mouths. But I'd be damned if I let anyone make her out to be the villain when that couldn't have been further from the truth. You want to label me an ungrateful son, go for it. See if I care. But there isn't anything I won't do to protect her."

Just when I thought this guy couldn't possibly get any better, he said something like that. "Did your father at least take the hint after that?"

Tanner's grin had a vindictive gleam I couldn't fault him for. "Not right away, but after I spoke out and revealed him for the lousy piece of shit he was, no other rag would pay him a dime for another story. The cash dried up fast, and he bailed again. No clue where, I only know I don't give a single damn if I never see him again."

I didn't blame him one damn bit. "That's why Luke is so protective of you," I guessed.

"Mostly. There have been other people in the past who tried using me."

"You mean women."

"You catch one woman poking holes in your condoms, another trying to sneak naked photos of you, and *another* who steals your shit to sell online, you tend to get a little jaded."

My jaw hinged open. "There are women who actually did that to you?"

He nodded grimly. "Yep. There's no lengths some people won't go to for a little cash."

I leaned forward, placing my hand on his knee. "Tanner, I need you to know I would never do something like that. *Never*. Not to anyone. I've worked really hard for everything I have today. It might not be on the same level as what you have, but I'm happy with me, and I'm not looking for any shortcuts. It feels good to know I've earned it myself."

He brought one hand up and placed his palm on the side of my neck, brushing his thumb across my jawline. "I know you wouldn't, Sunshine. I believe you." He let out a self-deprecating laugh. "I know it probably sounds crazy, given my history and the fact that we still hardly know each other. But . . . I trust you. I don't understand it, and everyone else might think I'm crazy, but I trust you."

The smile that overtook my face pulled so wide it pinched my cheeks. But I didn't care. "I trust you too." I might end up regretting that decision in the future, but that was another thing I planned to worry about later. Right now, I was content in my happy little bubble.

He leaned in for a kiss, but before our lips could make contact my phone started ringing. "Shoot." I forced myself to pull back and scanned the area for my purse. "I'm sorry, I have to get that. That's the ringtone for the store," I stated as I hopped off the stool and went in search of my bag. It was sitting on the table by the entryway, and sure enough, when I pulled it out, I saw my manager, Denise's name flashing across the screen. She knew today was supposed to be my day off, so if she was calling, she had good reason.

"Hey, D. What's up?"

"Sorry to call you when you should be relaxing, but Bethany has the stomach flu. I would have called Cara, but she's got her cousin's wedding out of town."

"Damn, that's right." I reached up, pressing my fingers to my forehead and massaging the tension away. "Okay, I'll be there as soon as possible. You good to hold down the fort until then?"

"Of course. And, again, I'm really sorry to call you in on your day off."

"No, don't apologize. I'll get there as fast as I can. And maybe it's time we start looking into hiring another person or two."

"It's like you're reading my mind," Denise said with a giant amount of relief. "See you soon, Boss Lady."

I disconnected the call and turned back toward the kitchen to see Tanner standing there. My face pulled into a wince. "I'm really sorry, but we're down two girls, so I'm needed at the shop."

He walked toward me in a way that reminded me of a panther, his movements sleek and hypnotic. His hands came up on either side of my neck, and he used his thumbs to tip my chin back so we were eye to eye. I *really* liked how he touched me. "Don't apologize. You're a successful business owner. This is par for the course. I'll take you home."

As much as I didn't want to leave Tanner's luxurious cabin mansion in the woods, I needed to get back to real life.

Chapter Fourteen

Tanner

As much as I would have loved to spend the entire day with Holly—most of that time being in bed—I got that she had a life and responsibilities and other people. I might have felt a neediness when it came to this woman I'd never felt before, but I wouldn't be *that* guy. The kind of guy who would monopolize all her time and want to be the center of everything. I'd known plenty of people like that. Hell, I'd dated women who acted like that. Who expected me to dump everyone else in my life and make it all about them.

It was a toxic trait I didn't abide by in others, and I refused to behave that way myself.

The silence that filled my car as I drove us back into town wasn't awkward or uncomfortable. It was the opposite, in fact. It was two people comfortable enough with each other that they didn't need to fill the silence.

At least that was the case until her phone started chirping.

She pulled her hand from mine, placing it on her knee—I couldn't be this close to her and *not* touch her— and leaned forward to pull it from her purse. The vibe coming off her changed as soon as she saw whatever was on it. The atmosphere that was light and easy just a second ago was now suddenly thick with tension. Hell, even the muscles in her leg locked up tight beneath my palm.

"Everything good, Sunshine?"

She jolted at the sound of my voice, like she'd gotten lost in thought and forgot I was even there. "What? Oh, yeah. Yeah, it's fine," she said distractedly.

It was the first time I could say with certainty she was lying. Whatever was on that phone rattled her, and she didn't want me to know. She hit the button on the side of the phone to black out the screen, then shoved it back into her bag. On a deep inhale, she sat back and offered me a little-too-bright-to-be-real smile.

"Just a spam text." She attempted to sound casual,

but it didn't ring true. "I need to get one of those blocker apps to catch them before they can come through."

I had to remind myself even though it might have felt like I'd known her forever, that wasn't actually true. If Luke were here he'd be the first to remind me of that little fact.

After she guided me around the building to the parking area, I pulled into a spot close to the door and killed the engine.

"I'll get that," I said when she reached for the door handle. "You just sit tight."

I climbed out and rounded the hood quickly, pulling the door open for her. The smile she was wearing hit me in the solar plexus. It was so damn beautiful it nearly knocked the breath from my lungs.

She took my offered hand, and I helped her down onto the pavement. "You didn't have to do that."

"Please. If my mom knew I let you open your own door, she'd skin my ass alive. Then she'd probably send Andrew to finish me off." My mother had instilled manners and chivalry in me as far back as I could remember, and most of her lessons still stuck with me today.

"Oh?" Holly arched her brow as she leaned into me, pressing her tiny hands into my chest as she grinned at me. And just like that, any concerns I had earlier were gone. "Now I'm curious. What were some of the other things she taught you?"

Wrapping my arms around her was as easy as breathing. "Well, let's see." I thought over all the lessons she taught me growing up. "Always take the side closest to the street whenever walking on the sidewalk. Always hold the door and let the woman enter first. Oh, and the most important one. The woman is always right." My mouth stretched into a wide smile. "Even when she isn't."

Holly's head fell back on a laugh, her spine arching as I held on to her. Her tits pressed against my chest, causing my dick to stir. Then again, there wasn't much she did that didn't cause that reaction.

"Your mother is an incredibly smart woman."

"That she is. She'll love to hear you said so."

Her cheeks pinched as her smile grew. "You're going to tell your mom about me?"

It was taking everything I had not to go completely hard. "I see you like the thought of that."

She attempted a mild shrug, but anyone would have seen right through it. "It's only fair. I mean, my whole family lives here. Our grapevine is faster than a race-horse on speed. The ones that don't already know about the date will soon enough. Your mom knowing about me would put us on equal footing."

I nodded, humming in agreement, but that wasn't why I planned to tell her about Holly. I was going to tell my mom about her because I shared the important things in my life with the woman who raised me. And something in my gut kept telling me that Holiday Bradbury was quickly on her way to being very important.

I bent my head closer to hers, cradling her neck and using my thumb to tilt her face up to mine so I could press my lips to hers. She made it hard as hell to keep the kiss chaste when she parted her lips and swiped her tongue across my bottom lip. I fisted the hair at the nape of her neck and deepened the kiss, unable to help myself. I forced myself to break the kiss before it could get too heated and I ended up fucking her in the alleyway behind her bookshop.

A pained groan rumbled in my chest as I took a step back. I had to fist my hands and stuff them in my pockets to keep from reaching for her again. The only thing that helped was that Holly was in just as much pain as I was. Or at least that was what I assumed from the little whimper she let out and the way her bottom lip stuck out in a pout.

"Christ, you make me lose my head."

"I know the feeling," she whispered back, and I could have sworn that my poor dick had a heartbeat.

"All right, baby. Get to work. I'll talk to you later, yeah?"

She popped up on her tiptoes and pressed one last kiss to my lips before she started walking backward. "Absolutely. Have a good day."

I could have headed back to the cabin, but I didn't feel like going back to that quiet. I had no problem being alone, but after spending the last several hours in that house with Holly, the thought of going there without her wasn't sitting too well.

Climbing behind the wheel of my Range Rover, I headed out of the alley toward the local grocery store, one of the things I enjoyed about Hope Valley. You didn't see any big box stores or chain fast food places. This town was run by the people, from the locally owned grocery store, to the restaurants, to the shops, and I was all about supporting anything locally owned and operated.

As I pushed my cart through the aisles, it hit me that this was the first time I'd stepped into a grocery store in a really long time. The cabin had been stocked when I showed up, and in D.C. it was easier to use an app and have my groceries delivered. I'd shopped for myself a few times after joining the Rebels, but it didn't take long to realize it was mistake. It took twice as long as it should have to get a couple of things because there was a hockey fan around every corner. If I wasn't being stopped by people who loved the team, it was people who wanted to critique every move I made on the ice and tell me how to do my job. It was just easier not to have to deal with it.

But wandering through Fresh Foods was a totally different experience. People waved as I passed, offering smiles or hellos. A few even addressed me by name. But the vibe was more like I was one of them, not that I was some hotshot athlete they wanted a selfie with.

I had to admit, it was really nice.

Since no one was being intrusive, I took my time, scanning the shelves for things that Holly would hope-fully like. I got the impression that wasn't something the men in her past had done much of, which was a shame. I was thrilled when she told me it had been the best first date she ever had. But it made me want to find those asshole exes and beat some sense into them. That wasn't even the bare minimum, for Christ's sake.

But if something as simple as cooking for her made her happy, I'd do it as much as possible.

"Tanner Fine."

My head swiveled toward the sound of my name, and a smile instantly pulled at my face when I saw where it came from. "Zach Paulson." I took his offered hand and pulled him in for a slam on the back. "Good to see you, man." I met Zach on my first trip to Hope Valley when I stayed at the ranch's lodge he and his family ran. And it was his wedding I'd attended with Ivy. He'd been a rough and tumble cowboy and his bride was a high-society nepo-celebrity back in L.A. They met when she'd landed in some hot water and her parents shipped her off to work on a ranch to try and knock some sense into her. Not only did she find her work-ethic, she'd also met her husband.

He clapped me on the arm. "Hey, it's good to see you too. Heard you were back in town for a bit."

Something about that very last word made my stomach twist. "Yeah. I needed to get out of the city and Hope Valley was the very first place I thought of."

Zach stuffed his hands in the pocket of his jeans and rocked back on the heels of his boots. "Heard about the injury; I'm really sorry about that. It was a shitty situation, but you're doing better, right?"

That was the moment I realized I hadn't thought about my injury in a day and a half, when it was usually front and center in my brain all damn day. Holly Bradbury was the only thing running through my brain.

"Oh, yeah. I'm all good. And the truth is I needed the break." That sure as hell wasn't something I would have admitted a few months ago. Hockey had been my life for as long as I could remember. It was what I existed for. When that doctor told me I was out for the rest of the season, it had felt like the worst moment of my life, like nothing could ever be worse than that. But as more time passed, it was harder to ignore that I no longer needed those five extra minutes in the morning just to loosen my body up enough to climb out of bed, and I felt better, overall. I still felt my age—and maybe a few extra years tacked on—but I hadn't been popping ibuprofen like breath mints to take the edge off the pain.

"Well, as long as you're good."

"I am, thanks. What about you? How's married life?"

His grin was instant. His features softened as he gave his head a shake. "It's the best, no other way to describe it. And I don't know if anyone's told you yet, but Rae's pregnant."

My eyes widened and I clapped him on the shoulder. "That's awesome, man. I'm really happy for you both."

"Thanks. We're pretty excited ourselves. She's due in the spring. Don't know if you'll still be here by then, but if so, maybe you'll get to meet the little sprout."

I didn't know if I'd be here either. The idea that I wouldn't sat heavy like a brick in my stomach, though. "I'd like that."

"Same. We're always happy to have you back." He shot me a wry smile. "Word around town is there's one resident in particular that's *very* happy to have you back."

Christ, I was a grown-ass man knocking on the door to forty, and I could feel the heat rush to my cheeks. "Holly's an incredible woman."

"I know. We all do. Which is why I feel like I should tell you, you screw with her, there are at least twenty people willing to bust your kneecaps and more than double that who'd make you suffer without committing a felony."

I should have been scared. Okay, I was a little scared, but more than that, I was happy to know Holly had so many people who cared about her. Those willing to commit felonies and otherwise. "You don't have to worry," I assured him, smiling as memories of my date with Holly began flipping through my brain. "I'd rather cut off my own damn arm than hurt her. She's . . . she's something really special."

His grin indicated I'd answered correctly. My knees were grateful, for sure. "Glad to hear it. You know, me and some of the guys have a monthly poker game, and this month's game is tonight. You should join us."

"That sounds good." A game did sound like a good

time, but so did spending time with Holly. "I'll see what Holly's got going on tonight and let you know."

We exchanged numbers in the middle of the canned goods aisle, then Zach had to get back to the ranch. But as I finished my shopping, I realized I was starting to feel like maybe this was where I belonged.

Which meant I was going to have to make some tough decisions really soon.

Chapter Fifteen

Holiday

I should have been in the best mood after such an incredible night—and morning—but I should have known there was another shoe and that it was bound to drop. And that shoe came in the form of a text message from a person I want nothing to do with. I'd been at One More Chapter, my safe place, for three hours, and all I could think about was that message.

I need five grand. You don't want to know what I'll do if you don't give it to me.

I didn't know why the hell she assumed I had all this money laying around. Like I could simply write a check and call it a day. Five thousand dollars would eat into a large chunk of my savings, and at the rate she kept demanding cash, I was going to be drained completely. But that wasn't the only reason I didn't want to pay up. The main motivation behind ignoring her was that she hadn't done a damn thing in my entire life to deserve what she felt she was owed. And it was that reason that really stuck in my craw; my low simmer of anger became a blazing inferno when it came to her.

Once again, the thought to block her popped into my head. But I couldn't. And the reasons were so much greater than my disdain for the woman.

"Hello? Earth to Holly. You in there?"

I blinked back into the present as Denise waved her hand in front of my face. "I'm so sorry. I totally spaced. What where you saying?"

"I was asking about the date." A cheeky smile stretched across her face, so wide it was a wonder her cheeks didn't split in half. "But maybe that's why you're so spacey right now, huh? Because you're thinking about a certain goalie who's built like a brick wall?" She waggled her eyebrows for emphasis.

I wished that was what was occupying my mind.

Choosing to push down all the bad, I brought the good back to the forefront of my mind. I'd had the best date of my life the night before. I was in my shop, my favorite place on Earth. And I'd been sexed up better in the twelve hours I was with Tanner than I had in the past twelve years. I wasn't going to let any person ruin that.

"The date was good," I answered, casting my eyes down to the counter as a warm blush spread across my face and neck.

"Oh, I know that look," she said teasingly as the bell over the door chimed with a new customer. "That's the look of a woman whose date was a hell of a lot better than *good*."

"Oh good! You haven't started yet." Denise and I turned to find Lennix standing inside One More Chapter, her foster son, Toby, at her side. "I want to hear all about this."

Toby looked at her with his brows pinched into a frown. "I thought we were here to get me a book."

Lennix reached up and ruffed the boy's overlong hair. "That too, seeing as you just informed me about a book report that's due in a few days." She arched a brow, giving the boy a scolding look, making the tips of his ears turn pink as he looked at her guiltily. But I couldn't miss the smile he was trying desperately to keep at bay. "I said I was sorry about that," he whined, the corners of his mouth quivering with humor, and I couldn't help but smile at their interaction.

Toby had fallen into Raylan and Lennix's unit like

he was meant to be there all along. Watching them together warmed my heart, and the rest of us Bradbury's already considered him one of ours. He was part of the family, even though Lennix and Raylan were still going through the adoption procedures. A piece of paper signed by a judge didn't matter to us one damn bit.

"What trouble are you getting yourself into now, nephew?" I asked teasingly, holding my arms open for him to walk into so I could give him a big squeeze.

"Hey, Aunt Holly." I loved hearing those two words come from him as much as I did from Sunny's kiddos and Rhodes's step-kids. He took a step back and gave me a bashful grin. "I might have forgotten about a school project."

Lennix crossed her arms over her chest, the loud, brash, take-no-shit beauty I'd known and loved most of my life was in full-on mom mode. It was something to behold. "Ah, ah. You're leaving something out."

My gaze ping-ponged between them before settling on Toby. I lifted my brows in silent question.

"The project's a quarter of my final grade," he muttered.

"That's right." Lennix came closer, leaning her hip on the counter and giving me her full attention. "He's known about this book report for three weeks now, but put it off until the last minute. Now he has to read a whole book and write a paper in less than a week."

He lifted his shoulders in an unrepentant shrug. "Bro, I've been busy," he declared.

Lennix's eyes widened. "*Bro*, you're twelve years old. What else do you have going on that's so important?"

"Well, we just got those new baby goats," he answered. "And Raylan and I are buildin' that treehouse."

That sounded about right. Raylan had passed his love of the outdoors to Toby, that was for sure. It was more common to find those two outside, wandering around their ranch, than inside. They fished and hiked and rode horses. Lennix had been rescuing animals in need for as long as I could remember, and, with Raylan and Toby with her, her menagerie had grown by leaps and bounds.

Lennix rolled her eyes but stayed silent, knowing that arguing was pointless. "Just go pick a book, will you?" Toby started toward the shelves, Lennix's voice calling after. "And nothing with pictures! You know the rules." My brows lifted toward my hairline causing her to roll her eyes. "Something tells me comics and graphic novels won't pass muster with the school."

"Hmm, you're probably right."

She flapped her hand like she was waving off that particular topic. "But enough about that." She twisted fully toward me and dropped her elbow onto the counter, propping her hand in her chin with eager eyes. "How was last night? I want to know *everything*."

That damn blush came back, giving me away.

Denise spoke up before I could find my words. "Didn't I notice you sneaking in the back earlier? Or did I see it wrong?"

Lennix's eyes bugged out with excitement. "What was she wearing?" she asked my manager, not even bothering to hide her nosiness.

"Um, a pink sweater, I think."

My friend sucked in a gasp so big, I was surprised she didn't suck all the air out of the building. "A pink sweater, you say?" She slowly swiveled her head in my direction, a Joker-style grin on her face.

The door opened again, setting the bell off. "Oh good, you're here!" My sisters Sunny and Gypsy came rushing in with more of my friends on their heels. Naomi skipped in, followed by Rae, who was preceded by her baby bump that seemed to be getting bigger by the day.

I rolled my eyes at the ceiling on a laugh. I should have expected they wouldn't wait for me to come to them. I wouldn't have been surprised if the entire town already knew about my date.

"You guys are just in time," Lennix said with a grin like the cat who just had an entire bowlful of cream. "Holly was just about to tell us why Denise caught her sneaking in the back this morning in the same clothes we helped her pick out *yesterday*."

My friends and family all made sounds of shock that more accurately belonged in a telenovela. "All right, all right. No need for pearl clutching. We're all adults here."

"Ooh, you little hussy!" Naomi squealed, skipping up to me and bumping her shoulder against mine. "Got you some!"

Rae plopped down in the plush chair closest to the register, propping her feet up on the matching ottoman. She fished around in her giant purse and pulled out a gallon-sized plastic bag filled to the top with her current pregnancy craving, chocolate covered raisins. Reaching inside, she snatched up a handful and stuffed them in her mouth. "How was the sex?" she asked, the words coming out a garbled mess around the wad of candy she was chewing.

"Yes, that." Lennix snapped her finger and pointed at her sister-in-law. "That's what I want to know."

I let out a snort, sure they were joking, but when my

humor was met with silence and eager expressions, I realized I was not getting out of it. "I don't suppose you guys would let me get away with saying a lady doesn't kiss and tell?"

Gypsy blew out an exaggerated raspberry. "Not a chance."

"I'm not discussing my sex life with my big sister."

"So you *did* have sex," Naomi crowed victoriously.

My blush was so fierce I thought my entire body was about to go up in flames. "You really are pains in my ass," I grumbled. "We did. And it was the best I've ever had."

They lit up in a flurry of squeals. Their excitement for me was contagious, and I couldn't have fought down my giddy smile and girly giggle if I'd wanted to.

"Oh, honey. I'm so happy for you." Gypsy's arms rounded into me and squeezed tightly.

"You're happy for me that I had good sex?" I asked with an incredulous laugh.

"I'm open-minded. Still, I raised you, so I can do without any details. But that's not what I meant. What I'm happy about is that you met a man who treated you so well you're lit up like a Christmas tree right now. You look happy."

My brows pinched together in confusion and my head tipped to the side. "Gypsy, I *am* happy."

Her eyes skipped across my face like she was taking

every inch of it in, studying me for any signs I wasn't being completely truthful. "I know," she said softly. "I know you're happy. But this is different. You never lit up with any of those other guys. You'd be excited and hopeful, but afterward, a little of that would be dimmed, like you were settling because some expectations hadn't been met. You had that look last night, and today you could usher ships to land in the dark."

It felt like a million butterflies were fluttering around in my belly. She was right, and I hadn't realized I did that. "He was amazing," I admitted quietly, so only she could hear while our friends carried on conversations around us. "It wasn't the sex, Gypsy. Well, not *just* that." A teasing smile pulled at my lips. "Because, *oh my god!* But it was so much more than that. After watching me make my coffee this morning only one time, he made me a second cup exactly how I preferred it. And do you know what he planned for our date?" She shook her head, her eyes glittering and happy. "He took me to the *insane* cabin that's actually more of a mansion that he's renting and made dinner for me. Because he recalled when I mentioned how exhausting it was, running the shop day in and day out, and he wanted me to be comfortable."

"Wow." Gypsy and I turned to see we'd gathered the attention of the rest of the group. It was Denise who'd made that declaration, her jaw hinged open as she gaped at us. "Now *that's* a man."

"Right?" Naomi lifted a hand and fanned her face. "Good lord. He looks like that *and* cooks?"

"Like he's a classically trained chef," I replied just to throw gasoline on the fire. "And because he wasn't sure what I liked or if I had food allergies, he bought the stuff for two different dishes."

Lennix leaned farther into the counter. The ladies were waiting with bated breath for all the tea. "Shrimp with pasta that he made from scratch."

"You lucky bitch!" Naomi yelped. "God, I'd hate you if you weren't such an amazing person who deserves to be treated like a goddess."

I let out a laugh, my chest expanding and rising with happiness. "All right, you got what you wanted—minus the details." I pointed directly at Lennix, her bottom lip coming out in a pout. "Still, it was a first date. *And* he's only here on vacation. You guys need to remember that."

I needed to remember that. I was all for having fun with an incredible man, as long as I kept my head on straight. Otherwise I was careening headfirst into heartbreak.

The bells above the door went off again, followed by a familiar deep rasp that I felt in every molecule and nerve in my body. "I hope I'm not interrupting."

Goosebumps broke out on my arms at the sound. My core clenched and my nipples pinched into tight, hard peaks. I spun around, my face lighting up with a smile that made my cheeks ache. And just like that, the warning I'd given myself only seconds earlier was completely forgotten.

"Of course not," I insisted, moving toward him like I was a moth and he was the open flame. I was helpless to resist his draw. "What are you doing here?" My eyes bugged out at how that came off, and I immediately started to backpedal. "That's not what I meant, it's just, I'm surprised to see you. That's what I mean."

Tanner chuckled and my core pulsed. God, the man was addictive. "I hope it's a good surprise."

"The best," I answered sincerely. He lowered his head, and I didn't hesitate to rest my palms on the solid wall of his chest and rise up on my tiptoes for better reach. He closed the last few inches I couldn't and pressed his lips to mine. The growl that rattled through his chest dampened my panties and sent a shiver up my spine. It wasn't until one of those jerks behind us cleared their throat that I remembered we weren't alone. That was what he did to me. I had tunnel vision when it came to Tanner. He was all I could see.

I let out a mortified groan and dropped to my feet, thumping my forehead against Tanner's chest as my friends whistled and catcalled. "Ignore them. They were all dropped on their heads as babies."

Tanner's laugh was rich and masculine. "It's all right. And why I'm here is to give you this."

I realized then that his hands were full. His left was holding a familiar paper coffee cup, his right a white paper bag, both sporting the Muffin Top logo. My lips parted in surprise as I took the cup he extended to me. "You got me a coffee?"

He lifted the bag in his other hand. "And a cinnamon roll. I hope that's right. The lady at the coffee shop said this is what you preferred."

I caught sight of my oldest sister from the corner of my eye and twisted to better see her. Her eyes were locked on mine, and she lifted her clasped hands beneath her chin. Her expression softened as her gaze darted between the two of us.

Bringing the cup to my lips, I took a sip, my eyes widening at the flavors on my tongue. I let out a pleased moan and immediately sucked back another sip. "A pistachio latte?"

He looked almost nervous that he'd gotten it wrong as he said, "Another suggestion by the lady at the register. Is it right?"

"It's my favorite," I admitted without hesitation. "Both of them. Thank you so much."

His shoulder lifted in a carefree shrug. "It's no big deal. I thought you might need a midday boost."

That. When I told Gypsy it was more than just sex, right there was what I meant. He was thoughtful without even trying. Kind without realizing. I knew my judgement of people—men especially—could be wonky, but Tanner was proving himself to be a good man at every turn.

"It's a big deal to me," I said softly, looking at him and hoping he could read how much I meant it. "Thank you."

"Any time, Sunshine," he replied tenderly, then leaned in for another kiss. "I also wanted to swing by because I planned on asking if I could see you again tonight, but I ran into Zach at the store, and he invited me to this poker night he's hosting."

Before I could get a word out, Rae spoke up, her hand poised to shove another fistful of chocolate raisins into her mouth. "You tell my husband if he loses again he'll be sleeping in the barn tonight."

Tanner grinned and nodded in understanding. "Yes ma'am. And like I told him, congratulations on the little one." He tipped his chin toward her belly. "I'm excited for you both."

Her cheeks flushed under his attention. That was the effect he had. Even women in happy, healthy, loving relationships weren't immune to his brand of charm.

"Thanks," she said, then let out a girly giggle that caught her by surprise.

I cut my gaze to her, giving her a look that screamed *what the hell was that* before shifting my attention back to Tanner. "You should go. I think you'd have a great time." There was also the added benefit that perhaps if Tanner made a strong group of friends here he wouldn't want to leave.

"Okay, I will." He brought his hand up, placing it on the side of my neck. "But I'll text you. Maybe I can still see you if it gets out early enough?"

One corner of my mouth hooked upward. "I might be okay with that."

He hit me with a brilliant smile that I felt from the ends of my hair all the way to the tips of my toes. "Good. See you soon, then?"

I barely suppressed the shiver at the feel of his fingertips on my skin as he tucked my hair behind my ear. "Yep."

"All right, Sunshine. Enjoy the rest of your day."

"You too."

He went in for one last kiss, then took a couple steps back. "Ladies." He tipped his chin at my sisters and friends, then he left. The door closed behind him, and I watched as he passed by the windows, giving one last wave to me before he disappeared. When I finally turned back around, the only word that could accurately describe what my girls looked like just then was *gobsmacked.*

"Well ho-lee-shit." Denise slammed her hands down on her hips. "Can you get pregnant from the chemistry bouncing between two other people? Because if so, you guys just knocked up the whole damn room."

Chapter Sixteen

Tanner

"Ha ha! Full house, assholes. Read 'em and weep." Zach slapped his cards on the table and reached for the pile of chips in the center of the table.

"Not so fast." Conner laid his cards on the table slowly, fanning them out for added effect. "Sorry buddy," he said with an unrepentant smile. "Straight flush."

My head fell back on a deep belly laugh as the rest of the table erupted into laughter. Everyone except Zach, that was. I'd mentioned the threat his wife passed on through me at One More Chapter earlier that day, and from the queasy look on his face, I was starting to think she'd actually meant it.

"Don't worry, man. You'll get him the next hand," I assured him, reaching over to smack him on the back before taking a pull from my beer bottle.

The rest of the guys rounding out the table were Connor, the local vet, Hardin, Detective Tristan Fanning, and Rhodes and Raylan Bradbury.

It would have been a lie if I claimed I hadn't been a little nervous when I first showed up at Zach's place to play poker with him and some of his friends. Two of those friends just so happened to be Holly's older brothers, after all. This was my first time meeting Rhodes, but I'd been friendly with Raylan on my first trip to Hope Valley. While I stayed at the Lodge, he'd been the guide who took me out hiking and fishing and introduced me to some amazing spots that only the locals knew about.

But with word of my date with Holly, I wasn't sure if that friendliness was still on the table. So far, they'd both been friendly enough. It helped that I'd willingly lost a shitload of cash to them so far, but I couldn't shake the sensation that there was another shoe lingering nearby, and it was dangerously close to dropping.

"I better," Zach grumbled, scrubbing a hand over his weary expression, "'cause Rae isn't playin' around. She'll really make my ass sleep out in the barn." He took a pull from his beer, then grumbled, "She's done it before," under his breath.

Connor slapped the table on a loud bark of laughter. "Oh man! Was that the morning the other week I caught you climbing out of the hayloft before dawn?"

Zach scooped up the cards and began to shuffle aggressively as the rest of us cracked up. "Laugh it up, assholes. But you're each one step away from saying or doing the wrong thing and ending up right where I was."

"Hey, she's building a whole-ass human being from scratch with just her body," Connor said. "Far as I'm concerned, women have earned the right to be moody and not want to put up with our shit while they're pregnant." He took the cards Zach dealt and flipped them up to see. "I look at Silvie every morning and still can't believe the woman I love managed to make this perfect little thing that owns my heart and soul."

That twinge I felt when I bumped into the happy family at Muffin Top the other day came rushing right back. I never had any kind of paternal urge before. I couldn't see beyond hockey to even consider a family. But hearing Connor describe how he felt for his wife and daughter tugged at some invisible string that made my chest uncomfortably tight. Hell, listening to all of them talk about the lives they were building with their women made me, well, envious. That was a new experience for me, to say the least.

We played another couple hands, and between the

beers, the laughs, and the comradery, my guard was down. That was when it happened. Like they'd been planning it all along.

"So, Tanner Fine . . ." I glanced over at Rhodes as he looked me up and down like a person might stare at a bug through a microscope. "What are your intensions with my baby sister?"

"*Our* baby sister," Raylan stressed, leaning forward to brace his elbows. He crushed the empty can in front of him with his fist in an effort to look intimidating, and it took everything I had not to laugh.

"Dude, what are you trying to do?" Hardin asked, arching a brow and looking at his buddy like he'd just lost his mind.

"I'm trying to come off threatening," Raylan explained, waving his hand at him. "Shut up and let me do my brotherly duty, asshole."

I couldn't stop my grin from overtaking my face. Truth was, despite the height and weight I had on each of them, I loved that they didn't hesitate to defend their sister. I liked that Holly was surrounded by so many good people, people who looked out for her and would clearly stand between her and danger if necessary.

"My intentions," I started, thinking through my words to make sure I said the right thing, because I was pretty sure that if I told them one of my intentions was to give her as many orgasms as possible, they'd both deck me right in the face. "We've only been on one date, but as of right now, my intentions are to treat your sister with kindness and respect, to spoil her as much as she'll let me, and to make her laugh, because she looks beautiful whenever she does it and it's the prettiest sound I've ever heard."

Tristan's sharp whistle carried through Zach's large dining room, bouncing off the walls. "Damn, man. You can't say shit like that out loud."

My head tipped to the side in question. "Why not?"

"Because you'll make the rest of us look bad," Hardin declared. "You can't hog all the romance for yourself. The rest of us need some too."

Zach snorted and gave his head a shake. "Man, no amount of romantic gestures is gonna save your ass. Not with that face of yours."

In response, Hardin grabbed a handful of pretzels from the bowl beside him and chucked them at Zach's head. "If your ugly ass can land a woman like Rae, I think there's still hope for me."

When I shifted my attention back to Holly's brothers, my shoulders sank with relief at their expressions. They might not like their baby sister dating, but they were trusting me to do right by her. And I planned to do that very thing.

The game wrapped up about an hour later with Zach winning enough of his money back to save him from the barn, at least for one night.

I said my goodbyes, and as I stepped out of Zach's house, the foundation under my feet felt a little steadier, like I was building something here, in this town. Climbing behind the wheel of my Range Rover, I grabbed my cell from the cupholder where it had been stashed and tapped the screen to check my notifications.

There were two from my agent, the tone of each getting progressively more anxious as more time passed. I ignored those and scrolled to the one that made me smile.

SUNSHINE:

Hope you had fun tonight and didn't lose that hockey fortune.

I let out a chuckle and typed back a response.

ME:

Have no fear, the fortune is safe. What are you up to?

Those three dots immediately popped onto the screen and started hopping up and down as she typed. A few seconds later my phone dinged with a picture. Holly wore the biggest, brightest smile that I felt in my chest and in my dick all at once. Half her face was squished up against her cat's as she posed them both for a selfie.

Another message came through right after.

SUNSHINE:

Just hanging out with my best guy.

ME:

Your best guy, huh? Should I be jealous?

SUNSHINE:

Oh for sure. Yoda's my one and only.

My face started to ache from how hard I was smiling.

ME:

You realize his head's shaped like a triangle, right?

SUNSHINE:

How dare you! I'll have you know that triangle heads are a sign of genius.

The urge to be with her, to see that smile in person, to touch her. To feel her wrapped around me as I slid deep inside her. It was too great to ignore.

ME:

Can I see you?

There was a pause before her next message came through, and for a moment I thought that maybe I'd pushed too fast.

SUNSHINE:

Now?

ME:

Only if it's okay with you.

Those bubbles came and went, like she was typing and deleting over and over. I hadn't even realized I was holding my breath until she replied with one simple word. *Yes.*

It took everything in me to keep from slamming the pedal all the way to the floor so I could get to her faster. The last thing I needed was to take longer because I got my ass pulled over for speeding.

The closer I got to her apartment, the faster my heart raced. Eagerness thrummed inside me, making my skin feel like it was stretched extra tight over my bones. By the time I parked beside her SUV in the alley behind One More Chapter my blood was rushing through my veins and I could hear my heart beating like a pounding drum in my ears. I hit the button on the intercom system and the door immediately unlocked with a loud buzz.

I heard the creak of her door opening as I took the stairs two at a time. As soon as I hit the landing, she was there, standing in the open doorway, backlit by the lights from her apartment. The smile she was wearing was so brilliant, so goddamn beautiful, it stole my breath.

"Hi," she chirped brightly. "How was—"

I swallowed down the rest of her question, taking her face in my hands as soon as she was within reach and crashing my lips down on hers. That was what she did to me, I had no control over the way my body reacted.

Her mouth opened on a gasp of surprise, and I thrust my tongue inside, tangling it with hers. She tasted like honey and sunshine, and a tiny voice in the back of my head kept telling me I was never going to get enough.

The need for air forced me to break away, but I didn't go far. With one hand on her hip and the other cradling the back of her neck, I rested my forehead against hers and breathed her in.

She blinked up at me, and the glassy, dazed look in her eyes caused my dick to stir.

"Hi," I returned, my words moving between us in a quiet rumble.

I felt the brush of her lips as they curved up into

another stunning smile. "Hi back. That was quite the hello."

A low hum rattled in my throat. "Couldn't help myself. Not when you smile at me the way you were."

The smile in question grew even bigger. "How was I smiling at you?"

I sifted my fingers into her hair. "Like you were really happy to see me."

Her hands came up to my chest. Her fingers curved and her nails dug gently into my skin through my shirt. A tremor worked its way over my body as she lightly scratched her way up my chest to my shoulders before locking her fingers together at the back of my neck. It was like she was scratching an itch I didn't even realize I had.

"I am happy to see you." Her expression gentled. "I'm really glad you texted."

Hell, if that was all it took, I'd text her all damn day.

Actually, I was quickly coming to realize I'd do just about anything to see that smile and hear her say she was happy.

Chapter Seventeen

Holiday

Something about the way he kissed me, the way the pads of his fingers pressed into my skin like he was afraid I'd disappear into thin air . . . it all built up inside of me, like a thread coiling tighter and tighter, desperately close to snapping.

There was an urgency to the way he'd just kissed me. Like he couldn't have stopped himself even if the wellbeing of the planet was at stake. There was something thrilling about having that kind of effect on a man like Tanner Fine. A man who could more than likely have anyone he wanted. Supermodels, actresses . . . but it was this small-town bookshop owner who brought him to his knees.

It was more than that, though. None of the men I

dated in the past ever made me feel so desired. So . . .
needed. It was like I was air to Tanner, and I was quickly
starting to feel the same about him.

Tugging my bottom lip, I looked up at him from
beneath my lashes. "Do you want to come in?"

"I'd love very much to come in."

My yelp ricochetted off the walls, quickly turning
into a fit of giggles when Tanner lunged for me and
scooped me up. He moved so much faster than I
expected a man his size to move and I had to wrap my
arms and legs around him to keep steady. He marched
right into my apartment, kicking the door shut with a
resounding bang.

That sound might as well have been a gun blast
signaling the start of a race, because it set off something
in both of us that was downright primal. Sex with
Tanner was different, and not only because it was so
much better. Something was different in *me*. There was
no hesitation or inhibitions. Sex with Tanner made me
feel *free.* He made me feel safe enough to take what I
wanted. And what I wanted in that very moment
was him.

I sealed my mouth to his neck, something inside of
me dying to leave a mark on him. Something that I could
look at and have the fond reminder of how it got there.

"Fuck, you're wild tonight," he hissed out as I fisted

his hair and jerked his head back so I could get to his mouth. Tanner kept pace with me every step of the way, moving through my tiny apartment to the bedroom.

We managed to break apart long enough for him to strip us both naked, then he gave me a gentle shove and followed me onto the mattress. I felt like I was burning from the inside out as his weight pressed me deeper into the bed. My core throbbed, the emptiness creating an ache that was driving me out of my mind. I couldn't remember ever feeling so needy. So *alive*.

"I want you," Tanner panted as he peppered the skin of my throat and collarbones. "Christ, I can't stop wanting you."

A thrill ran through me at those words, sending a flood of arousal between my thighs. "Yes. Please." I writhed beneath him, my desperation growing so intense I felt like it could consume me at any second.

"Mm," he hummed wantonly as he cupped my breast in his large hand. "Does my good girl need something?"

God, I loved it when he talked like that.

Arching my neck, I drove my head deeper into the pillows as I wrapped my legs around his trim hips, digging my heels into his firm, round ass to try and get him closer. "I need you," I admitted without hesitation. "Please, Tanner."

Something moved over his features that I couldn't quite put my finger on. He looked euphoric and agonized at the same time. "Baby." That one word sounded like it was being ripped from him. "Can I take you bare?"

"What?" I asked, my brain too hazy to fully comprehend what he'd just asked.

"Tell me I can have you bare."

My brows pulled together. "But, you've already . . ."

"That first time was accidental. The heat of the moment. I don't want to do that with you. I want you to tell me it's okay." He squeezed his eyes closed, his forehead against mine. "Tell me I can feel you with nothing between us."

"Tanner," I breathed, my heart feeling like it was about to beat out of my chest. "I want you to fuck me. Nothing between us. I want to feel just you." Before he could respond or react, I decided to take what I wanted. Reaching between our bodies, I wrapped my fist around Tanner's cock, giving it a squeeze before guiding it right where I needed it to be.

"Ah, fuck," he said on a heavy gust, his breath fanning the hair around my temples and forehead. As soon as I notched the head of his cock into place, he started pushing inside me, stealing the breath right out of my lungs. "Is this what my good girl needs?"

"Yes," I hissed out, my eyes nearly rolling back in my head at the delicious stretch as he sank deeper and deeper. I wasn't sure I'd ever get used to his size—at least not in whatever amount of time we had before he went back home.

"Fucking hell." His lips curled back from his teeth on a hissed breath. "Nothing's ever felt as good as you." He pulled out and slammed back in as if to punctuate his point. My back arched at the power of this thrust, a moan of pleasure ripping from my throat. "*Yes!*" I cried out. "Just like that, Tanner. Don't stop." I fisted the covers beneath me so tightly it was a wonder I didn't tear it to shreds. Tanner felt like perfection. It had never been this good. Wrapping my legs around his waist, I locked my ankles behind his back and held on as tight as I could.

He fucked me at a pace that was almost brutal, his hips slamming against mine hard enough I wondered if it would leave bruises. And why did that idea turn me on so damn much?

"Your cunt's like a glove, baby." He panted out the words, his breathing becoming labored as he used my body like he was exorcizing something inside him, and I was the only thing that could help. "You have the prettiest fucking pussy. Has anyone ever told you that, Sunshine?"

I shook my head, my heart in my throat as everything inside of me began to tighten. Pressure built inside of me so intense I didn't know if I should be scared or bask in it. "No."

"Fucking idiots," he gritted out as a sheen of sweat built across his forehead. With one hand braced in the pillows beside my head, he reached up with the other and gripped the top of the headboard, using it as leverage to pound into me even harder, his pace relentless. "Didn't know what they had. But I know. I know, baby. I'll tell you every goddamn day."

"Oh, god, Tanner." My eyes widened as that coil inside me twisted tighter and tighter.

"You've got the most beautiful pussy. Fucking made. For. Me." Each word was punctuated by a thrust. On the last one, he planted himself as deep as he could go and rolled his hips in a circle, grinding against my clit. That was all it took to set me off. I came on a shout of his name and a whole slew of other unintelligible words

"Ah, *fuck!*" Tanner barked as I clamped down around him. Tanner moved, resting back on his haunches and pulled me close so I was still stretched out across the bed, but my hips were in his lap. "Hold on, baby." I did as he instructed, raising my arms over my head and locking my fingers around the headboard as he drove into me, over and over, each punishing thrust shaking my body and the bed. "Gonna come so goddamn hard. That's what you do to me." A second later, he swelled inside me, buried deep, and came on a feral shout. I felt each spurt as he came inside me unobstructed. Each twitch of his cock inside me as he emptied himself set off a wave of flutters, over and over until I felt like a raw nerve.

"Oh my god," I panted once I was able to pull air into my lungs and form words. "That was . . . *oh my god.*" That was the best I could do. "I think you just fucked me stupid, baby."

Tanner chuckled, the sound hoarser and gravellier than before. "Jesus, just look at you." His pupils were blown, the black swallowing up all that warm amber as his gaze dragged over my body.

"I look like a mess." But I couldn't be bothered to move. I was pretty sure my limbs wouldn't cooperate if I tried.

"No." He shook his head. "Not a mess."

I tugged my bottom lip between my teeth. "Then how do I look?"

His eyes drilled into me, like he was seeing so much more than what he should have. "You look like mine," he rasped. Those four words sent a shiver through me and made my heart turn over in my chest.

His eyes traveled down to where we were still

connected, something shifting over his features that turned the blood in my veins to lava. He shifted his hips, his cock slipping out of me and forcing a stuttered gasp into my lungs. My legs moved instinctively, my knees trying to close together, but Tanner brought his hands to my knees to stop me.

"Don't close yourself off from me," he said softly.

I curled my lips between my teeth and loosened my muscles, allowing him to spread my legs wide once again. I could feel him dripping from me and let out an audible breath when he reached between my legs and scooped it up, using his fingers to push his release back inside me. A whole new wave of flutters started inside me and my legs began to tremble. "Tanner." I let out a whimper and arched my back as his fingers continued to play between my thighs, riling me up all over again.

"Christ," he grunted. "You were made for me, weren't you?"

I think I might have been. I'd never been able to relinquish control and trust a man to provide my pleasure before. Tanner not only gave me that freedom, but he actually seemed to enjoy being that safe space for me.

And, *god*, there was something so thrilling about laying there, completely vulnerable to him, while he tried to keep his release inside my body for as long as possible. Like he belonged there.

A minute later, he climbed out of the bed, ordering me to stay put while he went to the bathroom to get a warm washcloth to clean me up. Once he finished, he tossed the rag in the hamper in my bathroom and came back to the bed, in all his naked, impeccably built glory.

He pulled the covers out from beneath me and flipped them down, climbing into the bed and wrapping his strong body around me before covering us back up. I instantly sank into him, feelings of warmth and security washing over me, making me content.

Tanner's lips moved across my bare shoulder and up my neck. "Can I stay here with you tonight?" he whispered against my ear.

I rolled over so I was facing him, looking up with a lazy, tired smile. He'd worn me out. "Of course. As long as you don't mind sharing a bed with Yoda." My little fluff monster chose that very moment to jump onto the foot of my bed. He let out one of his little meows that sound more like a whispered honk than an actual meow, and slowly padded his way toward us.

Tanner crooked his neck to get a better look at Yoda. "What was that sound he just made?"

I let out a giggle. "That was his meow."

His head twisted back to me. "That was not a meow."

"For him it was. It's just one of the many things that makes him so perfect."

Tanner let out a snort and reached out to give Yoda's head a scratch. That set him off to purring, and he began to circle around until he found the right spot. Which just so happened to be in the bend of Tanner's knees.

"Aw, look at that. He likes you." When he didn't respond to my teasing, I looked back at his face, and what I saw made my heart start doing cartwheels.

"I like you, Holly. I *really* like you."

Leaning in, I pressed a kiss to his lips as butterflies sprang to life in my belly. "I really like you too." That statement was followed by a yawn so big it stretched the corners of my mouth.

Tanner's chuckle filled my tiny bedroom as he pulled me flush against him and rested his head on the pillow. "Get some sleep, Sunshine."

"Okay." Settling into him once more, I rested my head on his shoulder and pulled in a breath, filling my lungs with the scent of fresh rain and clean linen. I didn't know what the hell kind of cologne he wore, but I needed to buy a whole damn case of the stuff. "Goodnight, Tanner."

"Goodnight, sweetheart."

The last thing I remembered was feeling his lips

against my forehead before I fell into the second-best sleep of my life.

Chapter Eighteen

Holiday

"Where did you learn to cook like a Michelin-star chef?" I asked Tanner as I snuggled closer into his side to fight off the chill in the air. The arm he had wrapped around my shoulders tightened, pulling me deeper into him as we strolled down the sidewalks of downtown Hope Valley. Tanner had surprised me earlier, showing up at the shop to take me to lunch. We hit up the diner, and now that I was comfortably full we were enjoying the beautiful sunny day, in spite of the cold, as he walked me back to work.

A couple weeks had passed since our first date, and each day had been better than the one before. We'd spent more nights together than apart, some at his rental and some at my place, but no matter where, the nights ended the same: with me wrapped in his safe embrace. The better I got to know the man, the more I discovered all there was to like. I was starting to think maybe my radar on men had been fixed. I was happy in a way I hadn't been in a long time, however, despite that, I felt like I had a huge sign over my head, counting down the time to when Tanner finally left.

I'd gotten really good at sticking my head in the sand over the past couple of weeks, though. I was living by the motto that if I didn't think about it, it wasn't real.

Tanner let out a snort and turned to press a kiss against my temple. "That's a bit of an exaggeration."

"Agree to disagree." He'd cooked for me at least five times, and each dish was something I would have gladly paid a hefty chunk of cash for. "You're secretly a world-famous chef, aren't you? Hockey's just your hobby."

He brushed his lips against my hair. "Nope, sorry to burst your bubble, but it's only hockey."

I wasn't buying it. "You had to have gone to cooking school."

"No cooking school," he answered, humor tinging his voice. "I learned most of it from my mom. But we used to love to watch cooking shows together; it was a guilty pleasure of ours. We'd binge the cooking networks, then we'd try to recreate our favorite recipes.

We both got really good." A fond smile tugged at his mouth as he stared off like he was sinking into a memory. "Andrew's always teasing her that she's trying to turn him into a fat old man."

The way his face changed every time he talked about them warmed my heart. His affection for them both was written all over his face, and he didn't care one damn bit. I understood completely because it was how I felt every time I mentioned my siblings.

"I love that for you." Tipping my face upward, I smiled at him. "I love that you and your mom had something special like that."

He bent, pressing his lips to mine in a kiss that, while quick, still packed quite a punch. "Thank you for saying that, Sunshine."

"Have you talked to her much since you've been here?" He gave me a nod. "We try to talk at least once a week. It's harder during the season, but I find a way to make it work. She might not live close anymore, but talking to her regularly helps with the whole missing her thing." He tipped his head to meet my gaze, something playful and bright swimming in them. "I told her all about you."

Hearing that made my belly flutter with nerves. What if she decided not to like me? What if she thought we were moving too fast and worried I was trying to trap her son like all those other women?

Tanner brought us to a stop in the middle of the sidewalk. Turning toward me, he placed his finger beneath my chin and tilted my head back so those warm amber eyes could scan my expression. "Your brain is spinning. I can see it in your eyes. What are you thinking about?"

I tugged on my bottom lip with my teeth. "Nothing . . ."

Something flashed over his features like realization dawning. "You're worried she won't like you."

I narrowed my eyes and scowled at the shit-eating grin that took over his face right after he said that. "You know, you don't have to smile about it."

He laughed openly, tugging me back against his side and setting us back into motion. "I'm sorry." The accompanying chuckle sure as hell didn't sound sorry. "You're just so cute when you're worrying over nonsense." I reached over, sliding my hand beneath his coat to pinch his side. My own smile bloomed at the high-pitched yelp he let out. "Jesus, you're a vicious little thing, aren't you?"

"You'd be wise not to forget it," I warned. "And it's not nonsense. It's totally rational to think your mom might not be a fan of the woman who let you in her pants the very first day she met you. Especially given your past with women trying to use you." If I were in his mother's shoes, I'd probably be warning him away from me.

"Well, first of all, I'm not running to tell her every time I get laid, so I left out the part about already getting into your pants."

I rolled my eyes good-naturedly at his teasing tone. "Well that was stupid, because I told all my friends and family about it. In great detail." His head whipped around to me, and I burst into laughter at his expression. "Oh my god, I'm just kidding!" I said through a fit of giggles. "You should see your face right now!"

He let out a playful growl and lunged, burying his face in my neck where he knew I was the most ticklish. By the time he finished his assault, the muscles in my stomach were aching from how hard I was laughing.

"That wasn't nice," he grumped as we rounded the corner onto the street One More Chapter was on. "But seriously, you have nothing to worry about, baby. She's already hinted about wanting to make a trip up to Hope Valley. She said it was to see me, but I know her, and she's excited by the thought of meeting you."

My eyes went wide. "She wants to meet me?"

Tanner's brows pinched together, his head tilting to the side. "You sound surprised."

"Because I am. I . . ." I sputtered for a few beats,

momentarily at a loss for words. "We've only been dating for two weeks." I took a breath as I searched for the courage to bring up the thought that had been plaguing me. "Aren't you worried that maybe we're moving a little fast?"

Something moved over his face at my question. The light in his eyes only moments ago darkened, and his features dulled. "Are you?"

My mouth opened, the words ready to spill out, but I forced myself to pause. To really think over the past couple of weeks. "No," I said with complete honesty. "Which is probably insane, right? From the outside looking in, we probably look like we're moving at warp speed."

My shoulders sagged with relief as some of that brightness returned. "I know what you mean. But I don't give a damn what anyone on the outside may think."

That little voice in the back of my head that insisted on being rational at all times reminded me we were probably taking things quickly because we both knew there was an expiration date on whatever it was we were doing. I was *really* starting to hate that stupid voice and her dumb logic.

Letting out an exhale, I leaned into him so we could continue on our way. "Well, if your mom comes for a visit, I'd love to meet her."

It wasn't a lie, really. I did want to meet the woman Tanner spoke of so fondly. She had to be incredible to have raised such a wonderful man. Still, that didn't mean I wouldn't be rattled with nerves.

We were coming up on Muffin Top when the glass door swung open and the last two people I wanted to see came walking out. Rebecca spotted me first, and the instant she did, her hand flew out and latched onto Blane's, lacing their fingers together. Her mouth started to twist with an arrogant sneer, but froze before it fully formed when she noticed who was walking beside me.

A moment later, Blane lifted his gaze from his phone, and he finally noticed me. "Holly," he said, surprise mixed with something that looked like guilt swept over his features. "Uh, hi."

"Blane," I replied, my expression and tone neutral.

His eyes cut to the side, focusing on Tanner, and I didn't miss the way he tried to puff out his chest and straighten his shoulders. Not that any of that would bring him anywhere close to Tanner's size. Actually, seeing the two men side by side for the first time, the differences between them glared as brightly as the sun. Beside Tanner's chiseled features and massive frame Blane looked . . . dull. Boring. Seeing it now, it was taking everything in me not to laugh.

I felt Tanner's body stiffen and his gaze on my

profile as I pasted on a grin that I hoped was pleasant enough. When I looked up at him, I could see the question written on his face. He knew who Blane was. I'd told him about my past history, and he was silently trying to make sure I was okay. With him at my side, I was more than okay.

"Blane, Rebecca, this is Tanner."

Blane's hand shot out. "Good to meet you. Huge fan. *Huge.*" It hit me just then that I'd totally forgotten that hockey was the only sport Blane watched. But when he was sitting on the couch in front of the television, there was no end to the criticism he threw at the screen. He loved to talk like he was an expert. He made it sound as if he could play better than the men paid millions to do so.

Instead of taking his hand, Tanner stared at it for a second like it was a bug he was considering squishing, but lifted his gaze back to Blane's face, arching a single brow until Blane slowly lowered his hand.

"You are?" I cocked my head to the side and gave him a sarcastic frown. "The way you always yelled at the screen, I thought you hated the sport. What was it you were always calling the players?" I snapped my fingers together. "That's right. Stupid, toothless meatheads barely a step up from cavemen. That's what you called them."

Tanner tried and failed to cover his laugh with a cough as Blane's entire face started to glow red as a tomato.

"I think you're remembering incorrectly," he said through gritted teeth. That was another thing he used to love to do. If they ever added gaslighting to the Olympics, Blane would walk away with every gold medal.

I let out a hum of mock thought. "Hmm, no. I don't think so."

By then, Rebecca's shock had worn off, and she went right back into bitch-mode, a regular state of affairs for her. She kept a white-knuckle grip on Blane's hand and pressed flush against his side. She rested her left hand on his chest, fingers splayed wide to show off her ring, like the sight of it was supposed to upset me. Truthfully, I couldn't give a single shit.

"We were just getting a little caffeine pick-me-up," she stated, her voice overly sweet and her smile fake. "We're taking our engagement photos this afternoon. Isn't that exciting?"

"So exciting."

Her smile fell at my dry tone, a bitchy pitch coming to her lips. I knew if we stayed for one more second, she'd try to get in a hit or two, and I'd officially reached my limit on conflict for the day. Hell, maybe even the week, given how twitchy it made me. I much preferred not to rock the boat. It was why Naomi was always telling me I was too nice.

"Well, you two have fun at your photo shoot, but I need to get back to work. See you around."

Without another word, I hooked my arm through Tanner's and guided him down the sidewalk without a backward glance.

"So . . ." he started after a few seconds of silence. "That's the ex, huh?"

I narrowed my eyes into a glare at the humor in his voice. "Don't judge."

He held his free hand up in surrender. "Hey, not judging. It's just . . . *that guy?*"

I jabbed my finger in his face. "That's judging!" He burst into laughter, making it hard for me to maintain my surly expression when all I wanted to do was laugh along with him. "Not every man can be an Adonis."

He hugged me tighter to his side. "Aw, Sunshine. Is that your way of telling me you think I'm hot?"

I rolled my eyes dramatically. "On second thought, maybe we are moving too fast. Maybe we should slow things down."

Tanner's brows slowly rose higher on his forehead, but the look in his eyes told me he knew I was full of it. "How slow are we talking?"

I tapped my chin in mock thought. "I was thinking all the way back to first base."

He mimed driving a knife into his chest. "You wound me," he said, throwing his head back dramatically. That was all it took for me to lose hold of my giggles, and they came spilling out.

It was moments like these that made it so easy to push down the looming pain I knew was coming. Because he made me so damn happy.

I wasn't ready to say it out loud—or even admit it to myself—but I was starting to worry that I'd already fallen too far, and there was no safeguarding my heart against what was to come.

Chapter Nineteen

Holiday

It had been a long day. Made even longer by the persistent ache behind my eyes at the top of my skull.

The pain had been there since I woke up that morning. I knew what it meant. Years of experience would do that. A migraine was coming. I'd been getting them since I was a little girl. I had a prescription for them, but I was bad about keeping it on me. Any other day, I could have run upstairs and taken it, but it was like the universe had chosen today to point and laugh before throwing one obstacle after another in my path.

The store was incredibly busy, thanks to a book signing we were hosting for a popular Virginia-based author. The line had started forming early that morning, and kept growing. On top of that, we'd had a steady stream of people coming in to browse and purchase books. There was also story hour we hosted in the children's section every two weeks. The volunteer we had for that had come down with the flu, and with Denise handling crowd control for the signing attendees, Cara manning the register, and Bethany restocking shelves that were emptying out faster than usual, I was the only one who could step in. It was that or deal with the mutiny that was bound to happen if the littles didn't get their story. And, my *god*, but those toddlers could be scary when they banded together for evil. But those tiny words on the pages, along with the brightly colored illustrations certainly hadn't helped.

Now it was too late. Even though things were starting to die down and I finally had a chance to get my medication, it wouldn't do me any good. The light sensitivity had reached the level that felt like needles were stabbing into my eyeballs. A ring of black had formed around my vision and was steadily getting thicker. Next would be the stiff neck, nausea, and my pulse banging in my temples with each pump of my heart.

A sheen of clammy sweat formed at my hairline and the base of my spine. The kind of sweat that came with a roiling stomach.

I was squinting at the register's screen, struggling to

make out the numbers and letters on the screen that seemed a million times brighter than usual, when Denise came up beside me and placed her hand on my arm.

"Holly, are you all right?"

I twisted my neck in her direction, the motion making my head swim. "What?"

Concern formed a line between her brows as they pulled together. "Are you okay? You look a little pale."

"Oh, yeah. No." I squeezed my eyes closed and reached up to massage my temples, praying for any kind of relief. I'd dealt with this enough times to know I wasn't long from needing a pitch black room, total silence, and a trashcan. "Migraine's coming on. That's all."

Sympathy washed over her features. She'd been with me long enough to have seen me go through this on more than one occasion. "God, honey. I'm sorry. Why don't you call it a day? Go upstairs and lie down."

I looked around the shop, still teaming with people.

"Hey. Don't worry about this. The signing's over, so things will be dying down shortly. The girls and I have the rest. You just take care of you."

I knew it was the migraine, but I found myself sniffling as my eyes grew a little watery. "You guys really are the best," I insisted. "I'd be lost without you."

"The feeling's mutual," Denise replied as she took

me by the shoulders and turned me toward the back. "Now go sleep this off. We'll see you back here once you're bright-eyed and bushytailed."

Reaching beneath the counter, I grabbed my purse and cellphone. With one last wave to my girls, I headed toward the back of the building, past the stockroom and breakroom, to the door that led to the tiny alcove up to my apartment. Gripping the banister tightly, I white-knuckled my way up the stairs, desperate for my bed. Only as soon as I reached the landing, I froze in place at the sight of my open front door.

I knew it wasn't the best habit, and it was something my siblings and Gypsy's husband, Marco, gave me constant shit about, but I tended to leave the door to my apartment unlocked. It wasn't the safest, sure, but you needed the code or had to buzz through the back door of the building, and the one to that led into the shop locked automatically as soon as it closed. No one should have been up here.

Thinking that maybe one of the girls wandered up for something, I slowly pushed it open, and my stomach dropped to the floor at my feet. The items that had been on the entryway table were now scattered across the floor and the table itself was knocked onto its side. A little farther in, I could see more destruction, and the very first thought to jump into my head was Yoda.

"Yoda?" I called out, moving farther into the space. Panic gripped my throat, its long fingers squeezing so tightly I struggled to breathe. "*Yoda!*"

I raced through my apartment, vaguely noting the destruction throughout as I searched for my little guy. "Yoda, it's okay. You're safe." I searched beneath the sofa cushion that had been yanked off the couch and tossed around, searching for him. "You can come out." I made the kissing sound that usually worked. The throbbing in my skull was all but forgotten as I grew more frantic with each passing second. "Please, baby." My voice quivered, tears filling my eyes and making my vision blur worse than the migraine. "Please. Come to Mommy, baby."

Standing in the middle of my living space, I gripped my hair in my fists and spun in circles, feeling helpless as the tears spilled onto my cheeks. That was when I heard it. That whispered honking noise that was distinctly Yoda. My heart lodged in my throat. "Call out again, baby. Momma's here."

The sound came again, and I didn't hesitate, moving as quickly as I could through the mess that was my apartment toward my bedroom. His honking meow came again, and I dropped to my knees at the side of the bed. The comforter and sheets had been ripped off and thrown around, but I couldn't have cared less in that moment. A smile split my face when I spotted him in the darkness beneath the bed. More tears fell, happy ones as I reached out and wiggled my fingers. "Hey, buddy. I'm here," I cooed softly. "Mommy's here. You can come out now."

He let out another meow and slowly crawled toward me on his belly. As soon as he was within reach, I scooped him up and hugged him to my chest tightly. "It's okay, it's okay." I repeated the words over and over, more to myself than to Yoda.

With the knowledge that he was safe, the pain in my skull came back ten-fold. Pushing Yoda off my lap, I crawled as fast as I could to the bathroom and emptied the contents of my stomach into the toilet.

The overhead lights made it feel like I was being stabbed in the temple. Once I was sure there was nothing left to come up, I slid onto the floor, thankful I'd just cleaned it as I curled into the fetal position; the cold tile was a temporary relief.

Yoda padded up to me, bumping his head against my arm. "I'm okay." I gave him a pat and forced myself up. "I'm okay, I promise. Mommy just needs a second to get her bearings."

It took far longer than it should have, but I managed to get to my feet and shuffle out of the bathroom. As badly as I needed my bed, I needed to assess the damage done to my apartment more. Fresh tears welled in my eyes as I took in the mess.

Broken picture frames and knickknacks, most everything had been thrown around, but at a cursory glance, it didn't look like anything had been stolen, aside from a little bit of cash and a few pieces of cheap jewelry I'd stashed in the now-shattered bowl on my coffee table. This wasn't a burglary. This was a message. And I knew exactly from who.

Only one person in my life would do something so petty and cruel. One person who knew damn good and well I wouldn't report their vandalism to the police because that would put the rest of my siblings in jeopardy from her vindictiveness. Hell, that was probably why she'd done it, because she knew I'd cave, just to keep her the hell away from them. She knew my silence was my way of keeping them safe from her venom.

There was no other choice, and that killed me.

Reaching into my back pocket, I pulled out my phone and scrolled through my text messages to the thread I had been trying desperately to ignore, hoping she'd go away. It was clearer than ever that wasn't going to happen.

Instead of typing, I hit the screen to call and brought it up to my ear. The shrill ring was like a knitting needle to my eardrum, and I counted three rings until the voice on the other side finally answered.

"Well, would you look at that. It's about goddamn time."

Closing my eyes, I pulled in a fortifying breath. "Mom." My voice was flat, void of any emotion.

"So my flesh and blood finally deigned to acknowledge my existence. About fuckin' time, you ungrateful little brat."

If there was anything that could make my migraine worse, it was the woman who bore me, then abandoned me without a backward glance. "What do you want?" I spit out, cutting right to the chase.

Her maniacal laugh carried through the speaker, the sound coming out gritty, like she smoked two packs a day. I wouldn't have been surprised if she did. "I'm guessing you got the little surprise I had my friend leave at your apartment, huh?"

I knew it had been her. The only silver lining I could find was the fact that she'd sent someone else to do her dirty work, meaning she probably—hopefully—wasn't in Hope Valley. "The fact you had one of your thugs trash your own daughter's apartment is a whole new low. Even for you."

"Yeah, well, I always get what I want, and what I want is the money I'm owed."

She wasn't owed a damn thing, but I'd discovered over the past year it was easier to give her what she wanted. It kept her from contacting my siblings. They'd all done so much for me already, this was the least I could do for them. Keeping this vile woman out of the happy lives they'd built for themselves.

"How much this time?" The words burned like acid coming up my throat.

"Ten grand."

I nearly threw up all over again. "I don't have ten thousand dollars. You need to be reasonable."

"Bullshit," she hissed. "You got that fancy-ass store. I know you gotta be making money, and I want my cut."

I nearly choked on my tongue. "I own a small-town bookstore. It's not like I head a Fortune 500 company or something. I don't have ten thousand." The pounding in my skull intensified. I'd officially reached the point where noise was enough to do me in. "The best I can do is five."

There was a moment of silence. "Fine. I expect to see it in my account tomorrow, or you'll see what happened today is the least I can do."

With that, she hung up.

I managed to find the strength to clean up the worst of the mess. Then I turned off all the lights, silenced my phone, and crawled into bed, curling around Yoda and shutting out the rest of the world.

Chapter Twenty

Tanner

I went to Holly's contact in my phone and tapped the screen for what felt like the millionth time. Just like all the times before, it went straight to voicemail.

The knots in my stomach twisted tighter every time her cheerful, melodic voice came through, asking me to leave a message.

I glanced at the clock on the mantel again. Holly was supposed to have been here over an hour ago for dinner, but she never showed and wasn't answering her phone.

I couldn't keep my concern at bay. A thousand different scenarios played through my head as I paced the floor like a caged animal, each one worse than the one before. Was she ghosting me? Had she been in some sort of accident? Is she in the hospital, hurt? And if so, would anyone bother letting me know?

I couldn't stay still for more than a handful of seconds at a time. When it all became too much, I did a quick Google Search for her store and pulled up the phone number.

My heart felt like it was lodged in my throat as I waited for someone, anyone, to answer.

"One More Chapter," a bright, chipper voice said into my ear. "This is Cara. How can I help you?"

I fisted my free hand, flexing and unflexing my fingers. "Yeah, hi. Is Holly there?"

"No, I'm sorry. She actually left a while ago. Is there anything I can help you with?"

It felt like my lungs were being squeezed in a vise. "Uh, no . . . thank you." I hung up and dropped my arm to my side like the phone in my hand was too heavy to keep up.

"Fuck it," I muttered to myself, then I stomped through the living room and into the kitchen, snatching my keys off the island and rushing out the door to my Range Rover.

I managed to shave a couple minutes off the drive time from the cabin on the outskirts of town to the shop in downtown Hope Valley.

I didn't bother parking out front since she wasn't at

the shop. Instead, I drove around to the back alley. The sight of her SUV parked in its normal spot only made my concern grow.

I killed the engine and climbed out, my long legs eating up the distance to the back door in no time. Holly had given me the code to the back door the week before, and I didn't hesitate to key it in. As soon as the door buzzer sounded, I grabbed the knob, jerked the door open, and rushed up the stairs.

Please let her be here. Please let her be all right.

As soon as I hit the landing, I pulled a steadying breath into my lungs before slowly blowing it past my lips, using the same breathing exercises I did every time I stood in the crease. It usually helped center me, to get my mind right and my focus on the puck, but right now, I needed to calm my racing heart.

I rapped my knuckles against the wood of her front door. "Holly?" I called out after a few seconds with no answer. I counted five heartbeats before knocking again. "Sunshine, it's Tanner. You here?"

I reached for the knob and tested it with a small twist. It turned with no problem, and I slowly eased it open farther. I leaned past the threshold, unable to see anything through the pitch black. I was a few steps into the apartment when Holly's strange looking cat appeared in front of me, letting out that short, quiet meow.

He wound around my feet, headbutting my ankle and demanding affection. I bent and gave him a scratch between his ears. "Hey, buddy. Is your momma around?"

He let out another meow, then moved deeper into the apartment, looking back at me like he expected me to follow. Which is exactly what I did.

The sun had gone down outside, so there was nothing but the faint glow of the streetlights below filtering through the large windows on the far wall.

I moved through the space, following Yoda through the living room and into the bedroom. There was just enough light coming through the bedroom windows to make out the person-sized lump in the middle of the bed.

I rushed over, bending over the bed and placing my hand on her shoulder. "Holly? Baby?"

She let out a pained whimper that gutted me. "Tanner?"

"Yeah, sweetheart. It's me. Are you okay?"

She shifted her head on the pillow and cracked one eye partway open. "Wha—"

"You haven't been answering your phone," I whispered. "I was worried when you didn't show up and I couldn't reach you." I reached over and brushed her hair back, noticing the clamminess on her skin. "Are you sick, Sunshine?"

She let out a little moan and slammed that one eye shut again, like she couldn't stand for it to be open, even that little bit. "Migraine."

My stomach sank at that single word. "Christ, baby. I'm so sorry. Is there anything I can do?" I asked, making sure to keep my voice low so I wouldn't cause her any more pain.

"Pills. In the medicine cabinet."

"I got you, baby. Don't worry." Determination coursed through my veins. I was going to take care of her. And I wasn't going to leave her side until she was better.

HOLIDAY

I WOKE UP SLOWLY, my brain feeling sluggish and my body feeling like I'd fallen out of a tree and hit every damn branch on the way down. That was how it usually went after a bad migraine. It usually took me a few days to get back to rights.

I took my time waking up all the way, stretching out my stiff limbs and slowly pushing up to sitting. I had no idea what time it was, but the sun was filtering through my window, the pale purple and pink of the sky indicating it might be early morning.

A sound from outside my bedroom caught my attention and got me moving. Shoving the covers off, I climbed out of bed. My legs wobbled slightly, and I gave myself a moment for my equilibrium to kick in. Once I was steady on my feet, I opened the bedroom door and stepped out to find Tanner in my living room.

He was moving around the space, cleaning up the rest of what I couldn't the night before. Yoda dogged his steps, letting out those adorable little honks I loved so much.

"No, buddy. I told you, you can't go in there. We have to let Momma sleep, she's not feeling good. You can see her when she wakes up."

Things from the night before were hazy, but seeing him started to clear the picture from the night before. I remembered Tanner coming into my bedroom and finding me curled up. He'd stayed this whole time, taking care of me, alternating between warm and cold compresses for my head. He even massaged my shoulders and the back of my neck to try and ease the tension.

"I'm awake. And you're cleaning?"

Tanner's head whipped around. Relief flashed across his expression, followed by a brilliant smile that made my belly feel warm and fuzzy. At the sound of my voice, Yoda came running over, butting up against my leg affectionately, like he was just as relieved as Tanner to see me.

"Hey." He looked around the space like he hadn't even realized he'd been doing it. "Oh, yeah. There was some broken glass and stuff. I didn't want you to cut yourself."

A pit formed in my stomach, and for the first time since I started this thing with Tanner, I lied. "Oh, yeah. I was a little unsteady when I got home. Bumped into stuff but wasn't feeling up to cleaning it up."

He moved to me, gently taking my cheeks in his hands. A crease formed between his brows as he studied me, scanning every inch. "You okay, sweetheart?"

I reached up, wrapping my fingers around his wrists and holding tight. "You stayed," I said in a whispered voice. My chest suddenly felt too tight, like there wasn't enough room to contain my swelling heart.

"Of course I stayed." He said it so easily. Like it was

expected, the least he could do. The last time I'd been watched over like this had been when I was still a kid living at home. Tanner didn't understand how much it meant to me that he'd stayed. That he'd taken care of me. To me, it was everything. "I wanted to help."

He rested his palm against the side of my neck and swept his thumb right below my bottom lip. That was becoming my favorite caress. I loved when he held me that way. It made me feel special. Like I really meant something. "I hated seeing you in pain." His gaze grew tender, that beautiful amber warming like they were sunbaked. "I care about you, Sunshine."

That was the moment I knew I was screwed, because I'd gone and fallen in love with a man I couldn't keep.

I swallowed down the lump of emotion that swelled up in my throat. "I care for you too," I replied, using a different four-letter word than the one I truly meant. "Thank you so much for staying and taking care of me."

He reached up with his other hand and feathered his fingertips along my hairline, tucking a lock of hair behind my ear. Concern flashed over his handsome face. "You okay?"

I smiled up at him. "Yeah, honey. I'm a lot better."

He didn't look like he believed me. "You sure? You're still a little pale."

God, this man. "That's normal. It usually takes a couple days to get back to rights fully."

His frown deepened. "Does this happen a lot?"

I lifted my shoulder in a shrug. "Not a lot, but regularly enough that I have a prescription for it. Yesterday was a bad one. Usually I can read the signs and I know when to take a pill, but yesterday got away from me and I wasn't able to take it in time."

"You don't keep your meds on you?" That frown morphed into a glower, and it almost looked like he was mad at me, and I had to clamp my lips between my teeth to keep my smile at bay.

"No. Because like I said, it doesn't happen a lot." I reached up and rubbed at the pinched skin between his brows. "You can go ahead and wipe that grumpy look off your face. It'll give you premature wrinkles."

"I don't care about wrinkles," he grumped. "I really hated seeing you hurting like that. I don't think I could handle seeing it again."

My heart squeezed, and I felt another piece of it break off and fly to him. If he kept going like this, he was going to have all of it. "Well, pain is a part of life. I'm pretty sure you know that, Mr. Hockey Star." I cupped his cheek. "But this, right here, it means a lot to me."

"Sunshine, if you haven't noticed already, *you* mean a lot to me."

Oh yeah. I was sunk for this man for sure. And I wasn't sure there was any way I could protect what was left of my heart from being crushed when he finally left.

Chapter Twenty-One

Tanner

Classic rock blared through my earbuds as my feet pounded against the forest floor. Dead leaves and twigs crunched beneath my sneakers as I pushed myself harder than I had since I got to Hope Valley a month and a half earlier. The cold sweat on my skin felt good, proof of the work I was putting in. I'd learned a long time ago to read my body, and I knew what it could handle. I was almost back to one hundred percent, and *damn*, did that feel good.

My breath came out in puffy clouds thanks to the low temperature, but seeing as my job required I work on ice, the cold wasn't a problem. It felt damn good to run again. To push my body in a way I hadn't been able to in months. And it helped that the scenery all around me was beautiful enough to take my breath away.

When I mentioned to Raylan I was looking for a few trails near the cabin I was renting, he had several suggestions, paths that cut through the dense forest and led up into the foothills. DC had absolutely nothing on the beauty of Hope Valley. It was damn near every-where you turned. The longer I stayed in this town, the more it was starting to feel like where I was supposed to be.

Coming down the incline from the foothills, I picked up the pace, running at a full-out sprint once the cabin came into view. As I rounded the side of the house toward the front, I saw an unfamiliar car.

I barely had a moment to wonder who it could be when a familiar voice called out. "Looks like all that cold mountain air's been agreeing with you, brother."

A huge smile broke out across my face as Luke rose from where he'd been sitting on the front porch steps. A laugh burst free, echoing through the trees. "What the hell are you doing here, man?" I asked as I pulled him in for a back-slapping hug. He returned it, giving my back a good few smacks before we broke apart. I grabbed his shoulders, giving him a little jostle to make sure he was real.

"What do you think I'm doing here? Someone

needed to check on your ass, make sure you haven't turned into some kind of crazy, reclusive mountain man up here."

I chuckled and gave his shoulder a light punch. "Didn't we just talk on the phone a few days ago? If I'd gone mountain man, you'd have known it."

He grinned and lifted his shoulder in a shrug. "Okay, fine. Maybe I missed your geriatric ass."

I let out another bark of laughter. "Geriatric, huh? I could still beat your ass any day of the week."

Luke's grin widened as he clapped me on the shoulder. "No doubt about it. Man, it's really good to see you."

"It's good to see you too. Really fucking good. How long are you here?"

"Just the weekend. We head to Tampa Monday." I would have been lying if I said I wasn't a little bummed it wouldn't be longer, but that was part of the job. Until the regular season ended, you were on the go more often than not. There wasn't much time off.

"Well, either way, I'm glad as hell you're here now."

"Glad to hear it. So how about you let me inside so my balls can defrost, huh?"

I let us both into the house and headed right for the kitchen, grabbing a bottle of water out of the fridge and sucking down half in a few gulps.

Luke was slower to come in behind me, his head on a

swivel as he took everything in. Dropping his duffle bag on the ground by the island, he let out a low whistle. "This is some place, man." He turned in a slow circle, his gaze pointed at the windows as he moved. "Views every-where you look."

I grabbed a second bottle and tossed it to him. "Tell me about it. Seems kind of unreal, right? Turns out, the owners of this place are moving across the country later this year, and they're looking to offload. I was thinking about making an offer."

Honestly, in the past month and a half, this place had started to feel more like a home to me than the apart-ment I had back in DC. I might have lived there longer, but in all those years, I never had the desire to make the place my own. It was cold and impersonal. This place was nothing but warmth.

He nodded, then moved to one of the stools around the island and took a seat, twisting his water bottle open and taking a swig. "Think you'd be stupid not to. Lord knows you have more than enough money to buy your-self a vacation home. Even a rustic mountain mansion in the middle of the woods," he teased.

The sip of water I'd just taken hardened and hit my stomach like a rock at the words *vacation home*, but I pushed the discomfort down for another time. "So, how are Alice and the kids?" I asked, shifting gears and guiding us to a new topic. "She still putting up with your ugly ass?"

Luke grinned and flipped me off. "Everyone's great. Alice made sure to remind me repeatedly to give you her love and to get your ass home soon."

I forced my mouth into a smile. "Send my love right back to her."

Luke's eyebrows lifted on his forehead, his grin turning knowing. "Don't think I didn't miss how you skated right around the second part of her message."

A chuckle worked its way up my throat. I should have known better. If there was one person aside from my mom I couldn't get shit past, it was Luke. He knew me too well.

"What can I say? I'm enjoying myself."

"I bet." His gaze returned to the windows. "I can see why you like it here so much. Saw it just driving through town. Couldn't get over all those mountains. Place kind of reminds me of being inside a snow globe."

"Yeah, it really does. And the people are great. They know exactly who I am, but they don't treat me any differently than anyone else. They couldn't care less what I do for a living. Gotta tell you, it's been a relief."

"Tired of all those adoring fans?"

I arched a brow. "You mean the fans who like to stop

me in the middle of the street and tell me what a fuck-up I am any time I miss a goal?"

He snorted, all too familiar with what I was talking about. He got it regularly as well. We all did. "Everyone's a critic." He finished off his water and underhanded the empty bottle into the recycling bin beside the trash can. "I'm glad you're feeling the love here, but I'm more interest in one specific person, not the whole town."

"Oh, I see how it is. You're not really here for me. You only came to meet Holly." Not that I minded. There wasn't a doubt in my mind she'd win him over in a matter of seconds. "If you want to meet her, just say so."

"I want to meet her," he said without hesitation. "McClusky and Lee are jealous as hell I'm going to meet her first."

There was no point in delaying their meeting. Luke could be a persistent asshole when he wanted to be. And when it came to the people he cared about, there was no stopping him. "All right," I gave my head a good-natured shake. "She's at her shop today, but I'll give her a call and set something up."

"Jesus," Luke grunted, scooping salsa onto another chip and shoving it into his mouth. "Have you tasted this shit?" he asked around the food in his mouth. He'd barely swallowed the last bite before cramming another into his mouth.

"How could I? You've been shoveling the stuff into your face so fast I haven't had a chance."

He didn't look the least bit apologetic as he stuffed another chip in. "This is the best salsa I've ever tasted." Another bite. "You think if I asked really nice, they'd give me a couple gallons of this stuff to take home?"

Dear lord. My best friend was going to send Holly running with the way he was eating. "You think you could cool it for five minutes? The last thing I want to do is have to Heimlich your ass because you choked on Mexican food during a short vacation you're not even supposed to be on."

He picked up another chip, shooting me an unrepentant look as he scraped the damn salsa bowl clean. "Cut me some slack, would you? You know we never get to eat like this during the season."

He was right. Eating during hockey season wasn't about enjoying food, it was about fueling us enough to get us through each game. Some of the guys stuck to a macrobiotic diet while we were playing, but we all made sure to eat as clean as possible. Alcohol was out of the question, so a meal like this was a real treat.

"At least close your damn mouth when you chew. And, for the love of God, stop talking with food in your mouth." I spotted a flash of something sunny out of the corner of my eye and turned just as Holly reached the hostess stand.

"Holy shit." The humor in Luke's voice had my head twisting back in his direction. "Look at you. You're fucking sprung, man."

I didn't bother denying it, mainly because it was true. Instead, I pushed to my feet, waving my hand to get her attention. The instant her eyes hit mine and that brilliant smile lit up her face, my blood heated and my cock twitched, desperate for her like it always was.

My lips turned up automatically in response to her own. It was always that way. The more time I spent with her, the more my own mood mirrored hers. That was why it was so fucking hard for me when she'd had that migraine the other week. Seeing her in pain like that nearly fucking gutted me.

"Hey, Sunshine." I reached for her as soon as she was close enough, pulling her against me so I could seal our mouths together. I managed to end the kiss before I could do what I *really* wanted and spread her out on the table so she could be my dinner, and when I finally pulled back, that pink blush I loved so much had bloomed on her cheeks.

"Hi back," she replied.

A throat cleared behind me, and I turned to shoot Luke a look that would have made most other people piss their pants. The bastard gave me a smug grin that I was tempted to punch off his stupid face.

"Holly, this pain in the ass is my best friend, Luke Christof. Luke, this is Holiday Bradbury."

Luke stood up, extending his hand to her. The charming smile he gave her made me want to hit him all over again. "It's really nice to meet you." He shot me a smug look. "I've heard a lot about you."

She shook his hand. "I've heard a lot about you too." Looking over her shoulder, she shot me a wink. "The fifth best player on the team, right?"

Luke made a choking sound, his eyes bugging out while I nearly fell over laughing. *Christ, this woman.* She undid me at every turn. What I felt for her only grew stronger every damn day. I'd never felt this way before, and I never wanted it to end.

"Oh, I like her." Luke chuckled, looking back to me. "You put her up to that?"

I shook my head, feeling proud as hell. "Nope, that was all her."

He let out a belly laugh. "Good to know. Should we sit?" he asked, waving a hand to the empty chair at our table.

"Oh, you know what?" Holly started once we'd all taken our seats. "We should get more salsa. It's the best you'll ever have. Trust me. It's so good they actually bottle it up and sell it."

I thought Luke was going to pass out from excitement. "You, Holiday Bradbury, have just become my favorite person."

She let out a giggle that sounded like wind chimes. "Glad to hear it. And you can call me Holly."

"Well, *Holly*. Why don't you point out something on the menu that's as good as this salsa? I don't know about you guys, but I'm starving."

DINNER WENT OFF WITHOUT A HITCH, and by the end of it, Luke and Holly were going back and forth, keeping each other in stitches. She told him stories about the more eccentric people in town, and he filled her full of embarrassing stories about me that might have pissed me off if my girl hadn't been smiling from ear to ear the entire time.

She'd won him over without even trying, just like I knew she would. After we finished our meal—a meal in which Luke ate so much he was groaning in misery—we walked Holly to her car. She insisted that Luke and I hang at the cabin without her, and while I wasn't exactly fond of the idea of sleeping without her, I appreciated that she wanted me to get in as much time with my friend as possible before he had to hit the road.

"Dear god. My stomach feels like it's split right down the middle," Luke complained as we climbed the cabin's front steps.

"No one said you had to order three different entrees. That was all you."

"Worth it," he grunted, patting his stomach. "I mean, that restaurant alone is worth a return trip."

I punched in the code for the front door lock and pushed it open, waving him ahead of me.

"Well, I'm glad you enjoyed it." I followed him into the living room where he collapsed onto the sofa.

I took the oversized chair near the fireplace and was about to ask him what he thought of Holly when he spoke. "You aren't coming back."

It wasn't a question so much as a statement. Letting out a heavy sigh, I scrubbed my hand down my face as ideas of what my future may look like spun around inside my head. "Nothing's set in stone yet."

He cut his eyes at me and snorted. "You're joking, right? Tan, you're in love with the woman."

I opened my mouth, to say what, I didn't know, but no words came.

"Buddy, it's written all over you. But if it's any consolation, I'm pretty damn sure she feels the same way about you."

That was a direct hit to the chest, and I had to reach up to massage my sternum. If I were being honest, that was something I'd worried about, but hearing him say that made me feel a hell of a lot better. I arched a brow as I took in the man who was more brother than best friend. "I half expected you to tell me I was insane and that we're moving way too fast."

Luke's head tilted to the side in thought. "Would it make a difference if that's what I thought?"

I didn't hesitate in answering. "Not one bit."

A slow grin curled the corners of his mouth. "Good. Because I don't think that. Every relationship is different, man. All you can do is go with the flow. Just because yours flows a little faster than someone else's, doesn't necessarily mean it's wrong."

Blowing out a heavy sigh, I dropped my head back against the chair, my gaze traveling to the wall of windows opposite me. From my seat, I could see the stars filling the dark sky. "I don't know, man. I know I need to decide sooner or later. Alan's losing his shit that I've been ignoring his calls and texts."

Luck snorted, waving the statement about my agent off. "Man, Alan can take a long walk off a short pier. At the end of the day, they're in it for the money, not for the good of their clients. You've said it yourself, you feel better physically than you have in years. Maybe that should tell you something."

Hearing him say that made it feel like a two-ton weight had been lifted off my chest. "So, what you're saying is you don't care if I don't come back."

His eyes bugged out. "Are you kidding? I'll be fucking devastated. So will Lee, and McClusky might actually cry. There's nothing I want more than playing on the same team 'til we're both old and gray, but we both know that's not how this career works. But truthfully, all I really want is to know you're happy, man. And if Holly makes you happy, that's all that matters to me. You've had a long career. A *good* career. We all know our time in this is limited, and you aren't exactly fresh and youthful." He chuckled when I flipped him off. "Her life's here, man. She's got her family and that bookstore. In hockey years, you're practically an old man."

"Are you getting to a point, or are you getting off on insulting me?"

He leaned forward, bracing his elbows on his knees, his expression growing solemn. "You have the chance at something real with that woman, man. Something big. If you don't retire and move here to be with that woman, you're an idiot, brother. Besides, it's not like you're going to lose any of us, and DC's only a few hours away."

"Thanks," I said, my throat suddenly feeling tight. That was the last thing I expected him to say, but it was exactly what I needed to hear.

"Hey, wisdom's my middle name. Who knows. Maybe when it's time for me to hang up my skates, I'll look into life coaching or self-help. I'm pretty good at this shit."

Chapter Twenty-Two

Holiday

The cue ball rolled across the green felt and bumped into the eight ball with a resounding clack sending it right into the corner pocket with a resounding *thunk*.

"You have *got* to be kidding me," Tanner declared loudly, an over-the-top glare that had me curling over with hysterical laughter. "I just got played, didn't I? You're a pool shark."

Lennix came up beside the table we were playing on, depositing another round of drinks. "She suckered you, huh?"

Tanner and I had officially been dating for a month and a half, and he'd insisted on celebrating by taking me out on a date. We'd had an amazing dinner at the Groves, the fanciest restaurant in the county. The food was delicious, but it was the ambiance that had kept the place in business for well over a decade and a half. The rustic cabin was tucked into the foothills, surrounded by trees from all sides. Gas lanterns lined the walkways and twinkle lights wrapped around the surrounding trees and spread out along the large outdoor patio. The place screamed romance. It was expensive as hell, so it wasn't a place I treated myself to often, and now that I'd gone with Tanner, I wasn't sure I'd ever be able to go back by myself.

After an incredible, romantic dinner with the man I'd managed to fall head over heels for, we'd decided to keep the good times rolling and headed to the Tap Room. A live band was playing, and the place was filled with friends and acquaintances. I couldn't remember the last time I'd had so much fun in one night. And most of that was attributed to the incredible man who was, in that very moment, scowling like someone had just pissed in his Cheerios.

The glare Tanner shot my bestie had a whole new round of giggles bubbling up in my throat. "Can you really sucker someone when you aren't even playing for money?"

At that, Lennix raised her brows, cocking out her

rounded hip and placing her hand on her waist. "Then what's got you so butthurt, big guy?"

I tugged my bottom lip between my teeth and bit down. "I think it's the fact that he spent the whole drive here bragging about what a great pool player he is." I shifted my gaze to Tanner, giving him a cocky smirk. "He went on and on, so I had no choice but to show him up."

Lennix slapped her thigh on a loud laugh. "Ha! Sucker. That's what you get for being so braggy. My girl here had to put you in your place."

Tanner's head whipped in my direction, his scowl still in place but with no heat behind it. In fact, those warm eyes of his were glittering with humor.

I shot him a wink before bracing the butt end of my pool cue on the floor and striking a pose. "Don't hate the player, honey. Hate the game." My words cut off on a yelp when Tanner moved at the speed of light, looping one of his strong arms around my waist like a steel band and lifting me off my feet, spinning me in a circle.

He kept me close when he finally put me back down. His eyes were warm and smiling as his hand came up to caress the side of my neck in that way I loved so much. "Hating you isn't possible, Sunshine," he said softly, but the words and the feeling behind them might as well have been blared through a megaphone by the way they pierced my chest.

"Oh my god. You two are the freaking cutest ever."

We'd both been lost in each other's gazes, clearly forgetting where we were and that we were surrounded by people. Tanner let out a pained groan, dropping his forehead to mine as I let out a quiet laugh. My arms circled his shoulders, and I raised on my tiptoes as he lowered his head enough for me to reach, pressing a kiss to his lips. It was soft and packed with emotion.

When we finally broke apart, I caught my friend's gaze, and my chest gave a squeeze at the happiness painted across her stunning features as she watched us. "*So happy for you, babe*," she mouthed before turning around and walking back toward the bar.

"You having fun, baby?" Tanner asked as he brushed my hair behind my ear.

A wave of emotion crashed into me, causing my heart to swell so big it felt like it couldn't fit in my chest. There wasn't enough space. Even my lungs felt compressed.

"Tanner," I breathed out, my feelings threatening to get the best of me. I'd been holding those three words for a while now, and I could feel them bubbling up inside me, crawling up my throat. "I . . ."

"What is it, baby?" His brows pulled together as his thumb dragged across my bottom lip. "You okay?"

I love you!

The words bounced around inside my head, so loud they made my ears ring. "I'm good. I just want to tell you . . ."

"Tell me what?" he asked with infinite patience.

Sharp whistles pierced the air, followed by the thrum of a guitar as the band started back up, but it was enough to burst the bubble that Tanner and I had been wrapped up in.

"I, uh, just that . . . I have to pee." I didn't fault him one bit for the look of utter confusion on his face. "Be right back," I blurted out, then I whipped around and hustled to the bathroom. As soon as the door closed behind me, I braced my palms on the counter and stared at my reflection.

"What the hell was that?" I hissed to myself. "You have to *pee*? Seriously? Way to chicken out, Bradbury."

The door creaked open, and a second later, Lennix stepped through, pushing the door closed behind her. "Hey, you okay? I saw you sprint in here like your ass was on fire."

"I . . . God, I don't know. I just freaked out."

Understanding blanketed her expression. "Because you're in love with him?"

I nodded in agreement, my lips pinched between my teeth. "I almost told him. Then I freaked out and ran in here like my ass was on fire. He probably thinks I've lost my mind."

"No, honey. I'm sure he thinks you have a bladder infection or something."

I shot her a look. "Not helping, Lenni."

She giggled, then sobered. "Sorry, sorry. I'll behave, I promise."

"Appreciated," I said flatly.

She crossed over to me, resting her hips against the counter beside me. "So what's the problem?"

My eyes bugged out at her question. "Wha—what's the problem? How about the fact that we haven't even been dating two months."

She shrugged like it was no big deal. "People fall in love on different timeframes all the time."

She had a point. But still. "Okay, then there's the small inconvenience of him living in a totally different state." I began pacing the length of the bathroom, raking my hand through my hair. "He's not staying, Lenni. His life is in DC. His job, his friends, everything that matters."

"I'd argue not everything," she stated, giving me a pointed look. "You're here, aren't you?"

"Yeah, but what if I'm not enough?"

Her eyes filled with sympathy. "You're enough, babe. Trust me. The way that man looks at you, it's written all over his face. You're *more* than enough."

"But—"

She held up a hand, cutting me off. "Look, you can keep spinning out like this, driving yourself crazy, or you can be honest with him. Tell him, how you feel."

"He's not staying," I repeated, moving to lean against the vanity at her side.

"Well, he won't if he doesn't think it's an option." She bumped her shoulder against mine. "Not telling him you love him isn't going to make the feelings go away. All it's going to do is leave you with all kinds of regrets."

Turning to look at her, I gave her a tiny smile. "Look at you, being all wise and stuff."

She blew out a dramatic sigh. "It's hard being this brilliant all the time, but it's my cross to bear." We both laughed, and I leaned over to rest my head on her shoulder. "Just talk to him," she said gently. "Tell him the truth. You'll never know what could happen otherwise."

"Okay." I pulled in a deep, fortifying breath, then blew it out past my lips. "I'll go talk to him."

"That's my girl." As I passed, she smacked me on the ass hard enough to make me yelp. "Go get that hockey stud, tiger."

I narrowed my eyes at her as I massaged my stinging butt cheek. "I'm going to get you back for that."

She shooed me out of the bathroom, taking me by the shoulders and forcing me out the door. "Less talky, more walky."

We separated at the mouth of the hall, her heading toward the bar while I went the opposite direction toward the pool tables. I breathed in for three counts, then out for three. "You got this, Bradbury," I muttered to myself. "You can do this. Just open your mouth and tell him the truth. That's all you have to do."

Just as I reached the two steps that led up to the section where the pool tables were, a flash of red caught my eye, and when I looked over, my heart fell right out of my chest and onto the ground at my feet.

A woman I didn't recognize was standing right in front of Tanner. No, that wasn't right. She was *pressed up against him*. Their bodies so close there wasn't even a chance of light getting through.

Their lips were moving as they spoke to one another, but I was too far away to make out the words. One thing was obvious though. The way he was looking at her, and the way she had her hands on him, they clearly knew each other. Intimately.

My lungs suddenly stopped working right, making it difficult to pull in a full breath. The pain that pierced my chest was worse than anything I'd ever experienced. Even that time I'd broken my arm when I was six.

I couldn't move. All I could do was stand there and stare as I bled out all over the floor. At least that was what it felt like.

I didn't think it was possible for the pain to get any worse, but I was quickly proven wrong when the redheaded woman lifted up on her toes and kissed Tanner, right there in the middle of the bar, in front of everyone. People I knew, friends, associates, watched on with gaping mouths, their gazes bouncing back and forth between where I stood, and where Tanner was in a clinch with a woman who was absolutely *not* me.

If I thought the humiliation at being cheated on by Blane was bad, it was nothing compared to having your heartbreak witnessed in real time by people you'd have to see day in and day out.

My sinuses began to burn and my vision grew blurry as tears welled up in my eyes, but I refused to blink. No way I was going to let them fall where Tanner and everyone else could see.

It happened in slow motion. Tanner clasped the woman's wrists and took a step back, his eyes lifting to meet mine. A myriad of emotions played over his expression before his lips formed my name. He released the woman quickly, like the feel of her skin burned him, and took a step toward me, but I quickly mirrored it, moving one pace back. I desperately needed to maintain distance between us, or I was going to break.

His voice rose over the din of noise in the bar, over the rush of blood in my ears. "Holly, it's not what it looks like—" he started, but I was done.

Turning on my heel, I rushed through the thick crowd of people toward the exit and away from Tanner.

Chapter Twenty-Three

Tanner

"Holly, wait!" I tried to go after her, but it was as if the crowd swallowed her up. Where it had parted for her, allowing her to make a quick escape, it crashed back together like a wave beating against a rocky cliff, making it almost impossible for me to get through.

I could feel the stares on me, and I was vaguely aware of the whispered voices and pissed-off looks directed at me, but in that moment, I could only focus on one thing. And that was the fact that my heart just ran away from me.

"Tanner. Tanner! I need to talk to you."

I whirled around on the woman who may have cost me everything. The look I shot her had her taking a step back. Smart, seeing as I didn't feel in control of myself just then. "What. The *fuck*. Was. That?" Each word cracked through the air like a gunshot.

Sandra at least had the decency to look nervous, her throat working on a swallow, as she took another step away. "I-I'm sorry. I just thought—"

I cut her off, my voice as hard and rigid as cold steel "No you didn't. You didn't fucking think at all. If you had, you would have stopped texting and calling when I told you we were done. You wouldn't have stalked me across state fucking lines. And you sure as shit wouldn't have touched me or kissed me when I gave you absolutely *zero* indication that was what I wanted!" My voice rose with each word until it was so loud it boomed over the jumble of noises blending together in the bar.

The color quickly leeched from Sandra's face. "But . . . we were so good together." It was the same shit she'd been spewing when she cornered me at the pool tables. I'd been so shocked to see her that my brain had momentarily glitched. That was the only reason she got close enough to put her hands on me . . . to kiss me. She'd taken my stunned state and used it to her advantage. "I just thought if I came here, if I reminded you, maybe you'd give me another shot."

"Sandra, we weren't anything more than an occasional hookup. We didn't have any kind of relationship."

Tears welled up in her eyes, but they had no effect. "Don't say that."

"It's the goddamn truth! We were never anything but casual. And I know that because I never once shared anything of substance with you. But that woman," I pointed toward the door, "the one who just ran out of here, she knows every single piece of me, because I gave that to her. And in one fucking breath, you may have destroyed that."

Movement from the corner of my eye caught my attention, and I turned just in time to see Lennix join our little huddle. Thunder rolled over her features, and if I wasn't already mad enough to breathe fire, it would have been enough to have me pissing myself. "Everything okay over here?"

"No," I answered immediately. "Everything is fucking far from okay. This woman stalked me all the way from DC, followed me to the bar, and after I told her she needed to leave, she kissed me. Right in front of Holly."

Her eyebrows shot up. "You consent to that kiss?"

I pinned Sandra in place with a murderous look. "Absolutely not."

"Tanner," Sandra breathed, but I was done listening to what she had to say.

Lennix let out a sharp whistle, then raised her arm in

the air, waving over the wall of muscle near the door wearing a shirt that read *Security.* "Zeke, please escort this woman off the premises, and make sure she doesn't return."

Sandra's jaw hinged open in an affronted gasp. "Wait. What?"

"She's kicking you out," I said on a hiss. I took one step toward her, pointing my finger in her face. "And let me make something perfectly clear. If I ever see your face again, if you ever text or call, if you even so much as breathe in my general direction, I will file a restraining order. You understand me? And I won't stop there," I warned, then I lowered my voice. "I didn't want to hurt you. I tried letting you down easy, but you wouldn't accept it. Now I'm done being nice. And listen to me when I tell you, I am not the man you want to fuck with. Test me and see what happens."

I didn't bother sparing her another glance as Zeke grabbed her by the bicep to remove her from the bar. She wasn't worth another second of my time. The only thing that mattered was getting to Holly.

I was sure a good number of cellphones had come out to record that encounter, and odds were, it would be on the internet in no time, but I couldn't find it in me to give a shit.

As I rushed out of the bar, the image of Holly's face

played in my mind on a continuous loop. The pain in her eyes, the hurt and betrayal, it was like a knife to the gut, stabbing over and over. I jumped behind the wheel of my Range Rover and threw it into gear, whipping out of the parking lot at a carelessly fast speed. If I wasn't careful, I was going to have an accident before I could find my girl, explain everything, then beg for her forgiveness.

I hit the button on my steering wheel to call Holly, but all it did was ring and ring, the shrill sound blasting through my speakers and stabbing onto my ears.

"Holly, baby, it's me," I spoke into the dark cab of the car as soon as I got her voicemail. "Please. Please call me back. What you saw, it isn't what it looked like. I swear. I can explain everything. Please just call me back."

I disconnected and tried again. That time, the phone didn't even ring before cutting over to voicemail. "Shit," I hissed, slamming my palm against the steering wheel. My stomach twisted violently as I raced through the streets toward her apartment.

I jerked the wheel hard, turning into the back alley so fast my tires squealed. The first thing I noticed was that her car wasn't in its usual spot, but that didn't stop me from slamming on the brakes and throwing the gearshift into park. I jumped out, not bothering to kill the ignition or shut the door, before racing toward the building. I keyed in the code, nearly ripping the door off the hinges as soon as it unlocked.

"Holly," I shouted as I raced up the stairs. "Holly, are you in there?" I called as I beat my knuckles against the wooden door. Nothing. I pressed my ear to the door, straining to hear anything on the other side, but all was quiet.

Pulling the phone from my back pocket, I hit her contact and held it down by my leg, listening to see if I could hear it ringing from the other side. There was no sound. There wasn't even any light coming from the crack near the floor.

Panic raced through my veins, making my blood burn as I took a stumbling step back and raked a hand through my hair violently. I didn't know what the hell to do. I couldn't remember a time when I'd felt so helpless. I was terrified I wouldn't find her. Or that, if I did, she wouldn't care to hear what I had to say. I didn't know what the hell to do or where to look for her. All I knew was that I couldn't lose her. The woman owned my heart, and if I lost her, if she ended us, I would never get it back.

Then an idea popped into my head. Lifting the phone back up, I scrolled through my contacts until I got to Raylan's name, and hit call. It rang twice before he answered.

"Already talked to Lennix, so if you're callin' to explain, you don't need to. It's all good."

"No, it's not," I croaked. "I can't find Holly. She's not at her apartment, and I don't know where the hell else to look." Squeezing my eyes closed, I let the pain wash over me. "Please tell me you have some idea where she might be."

Silence carried over the line for one beat, then two. By the third, I felt like I was going to come out of my skin. Then Raylan spoke. "There might be one place. I don't know if she still goes there, but it used to be where she went when she was hurting and needed space to put herself back together."

Desperation and hope warred against each other inside of me. "Tell me."

I PULLED up to the curb the GPS led me to, cutting off the engine and looking out the passenger window at the big, red brick house. According to Raylan, this was where their oldest sister, Gypsy, and her husband, Marco, lived. It was the house where Holly had spent most of her childhood and teenage years before moving out on her own.

All the windows were dark, and Raylan said the couple was out of town on a short vacation to the Outer Banks, but it was where I hoped to find the woman who held my heart in the palm of her hand.

Climbing out of the car, I headed up the driveway, going past the main house. I let out a sigh of relief when I spotted Holly's SUV in the driveway. Just like Raylan said, a gate led to the backyard. I punched in the code he'd given me to unlock it, and pushed it open. Past the backyard, a smaller structure butted up against the woods at the property line. It looked like a miniature version of the main house, and the windows were lit up with the warm glow of lights coming from the inside.

She was here, and she was safe. And I could only hope she would talk to me.

Chapter Twenty-Four

Holiday

Curling my knees tighter to my body, I pulled the throw blanket higher, tucking it under my chin and snuggling deeper into the squashy couch cushions, hoping this place would offer me the same calm and comfort that it always had in the past.

Before I bought One More Chapter and turned it into what it was now, this house had been where I went for comfort. For solace. It wasn't so much the actual house as the memories that came from my time spent here that always made me feel better.

This tiny house was where I went whenever someone picked on me at school, or when I caught my date at the Homecoming dance making out with Kelly

Martin beneath the school bleachers. This was where I went for every major milestone in my life after the age of six, when I needed to just be. To soak in all the good or push out all the bad.

That was why I was here now. I hoped it would work its usual magic on my battered and bruised heart. The problem was, it had never hurt the way it was hurting now.

I wriggled deeper into the back cushions, hoping to find the essence of the woman who lived here before.

With Gypsy and Marco gone and the main house empty, the silence was thicker than usual. I felt it pressing down on me, like it was trying to push my head under water.

It didn't help that I'd turned my cellphone off and left it in my car, but the damn thing wouldn't stop going off. Lennix and Tanner had been blowing it up, then my brother Raylan had joined in, and I couldn't stand the noise. I was starting to rethink my decision when a knock sounded on the carriage house's front door.

My head came off the arm of the couch, and I stared at the door with a frown, wondering who the hell it could be. I hadn't told anyone where I was going, so no one should be knocking on the door.

I started to think my mind was playing tricks on me, and maybe I didn't hear what I thought I heard, when another knock came. Only, that time, a familiar deep voice followed right after.

"I know you're in there, Sunshine. Please open the door." My mouth dropped open, but the words got stuck in my throat. "Baby, I know you're in there. Please. Just five minutes, and if you don't like what I have to say, I'll leave. I give you my word." Another beat of silence followed, and while I tried to decide what the hell I was going to do, the next words out of his mouth sealed my decision. "That's fine. If you won't answer, I'll just sleep out here on the front porch. I've slept in worse places. This'll be nothing."

Blowing out a sigh, I tossed the blanket aside and climbed to my feet. I didn't bother looking at the mirror in the entryway as I passed, because I knew I had to look a real mess. I'd cried off most of my mascara, and what was left was probably streaked down my cheeks. I knew without having to look that my face was all red and blotchy, and that the tip of my nose was swollen to twice its usual size. I was *not* a pretty crier. I used to envy the women in movies who all cried so femininely, a few clear tears dripping from their eyes, because that was so not me.

Twisting the deadbolt, I grabbed the knob and gave it a turn, pulling the door to the carriage house open. The sight in front of me had a whole new wave of tears welling up in my eyes. Tanner stood right there, across the threshold, looking *ravaged*. His eyes were bloodshot, his hair was in disarray, like he'd been pulling on it in frustration. His gaze was slightly manic, and I didn't miss the way he was gripping the doorframe so tightly his knuckles were bleached white, as though he had to hold himself back from reaching for me.

"What do you want?" I'd been hoping to sound strong, but my throat was raw from crying, and the words came out sounding like I'd gargled gravel.

His brows fell, devastation washing over his gorgeous face. "Sunshine," he croaked out. His Adam's apple bobbed on a thick swallow. "Can—can I touch you?"

God, I wanted that so badly. That request caused new tears to break free and spill down my cheeks. "I'd rather you didn't."

Without my permission, he didn't reach for me, but the war was written all over his face. "Holly, baby, please don't cry. You're tearing me apart."

Didn't he realize he was doing that very thing to me? I sniffed back the rest of my tears and cleared the roughness from my throat. "You said you wanted to explain, so explain."

A flicker of hope flashed across his face so fast I

nearly missed it. There and gone in the blink of an eye. "Can I at least come in?"

I didn't know what it said about me that I couldn't say no to that, but instead of questioning it, I simply stepped to the side to let him in.

The room suddenly felt like it shrank to half its size once Tanner was standing in it. It wasn't only his physical size that took up so much of the space, his presence did as well.

Closing the door, I moved back to the couch and sat down at one end, tucking my feet beneath me, and wrapping my arms around my waist in a protective hold. Instead of taking the chair across from me, he sat on the coffee table directly in front of me, leaning forward to rest his elbows on his knees and bringing himself so close I smelled the fresh rain scent on his skin. The heat radiating from him poured over me. It was as if every aspect of him was everywhere, all at once. There was no escaping him.

"Who is she?" I forced myself to ask, even though I didn't really want to know. If tonight had taught me anything, it was that the time for burying my head in the sand was long gone.

"She's someone I knew back in DC."

I swallowed down the lump that had formed in my throat and forced the words out. "A girlfriend?"

"No," he answered vehemently. "Not a girlfriend. She was never that. It was only ever casual between us. We'd both gone into it knowing that. She tried to make it more, but I was clear that wasn't going to happen. I eventually ended things for good when I caught her taking pictures of me."

My brows winged up in shock. "What kind of pictures?"

"In some of them, I'd just gotten out of the shower. In others I was only wearing underwear."

A chill worked its way down my spine. "And you didn't know she'd taken them?"

He shook his head, and all of a sudden, my blood began to boil. "She said she wasn't planning on doing anything with them, but I didn't believe her and made her delete them. Good thing too, because one of her friends met my teammate at a bar a few weeks later and told him Sandra planned to try to sell them to the highest bidder."

What a bitch! I was suddenly mad I ran out of the bar the way I did. After hearing this, I wanted to track her down and rip all that red hair out.

"But, I don't understand. If you two aren't together, what was she doing here? And why did you kiss her?"

"I didn't kiss her," he insisted. "I know it must have looked that way, but I didn't kiss her, Sunshine, I swear. I was shocked to see her. I froze for a moment and she took advantage of that. She kissed me, but I swear to you, I didn't want it, and I stopped it right away."

What he was describing started to make sense. He had been the one to step away, I'd seen that with my own eyes. Looking back on it now, I realize that, while they'd obviously known each other, I didn't see any indication that he was happy to see her.

"I don't know how the hell she found out where I was, because I sure as hell didn't tell her. And I know none of my teammates would either. After you ran out, I told her if I ever saw her face again, I'd file a restraining order. Then your friend Lennix had security throw her out. I didn't hang around to make sure she left. The only thing I could think was that I needed to get to you."

He reached out then, taking my hands in his, swiping his thumbs across the backs of them. "You have to believe me, I would never do anything to hurt you. Seeing the look on your face after she kissed me . . ." He trailed off, giving his head a shake as his eyes grew red all over again. "Fucking killed me, Holly," he said, the words coming out hoarse and raspy, like his throat was coated in sandpaper. "I never want to see that look on your face ever again, and sure as hell never want to be the cause of it." His fingers squeezed mine tighter. "I'd rather lose a goddamn limb."

My tongue came out, swiping across my lip before tugging it between my teeth. At my silence, desperation sparked in his gaze, setting that amber ablaze. "Say you believe me. Please, Sunshine, you have to believe me."

I felt the pieces of my heart knitting themselves back together, but even with the heartache easing, the fear was still there, as real as ever. "I believe you," I whispered.

I could practically see the relief coming off him as his shoulders slumped and his head dropped forward. "Thank you," he rasped, his gaze returning to mine a second later. "Thank you, baby. Can I hold you now? Please?"

I barely finished nodding when he moved. His strength still blew me away. The ease with which he lifted me off the couch so he could take my place, depositing me in his lap was unreal. As soon as his familiar warmth wrapped around me, every ounce of tension swept from my body, and I melted into him. Warm tears filled my eyes and dripped against his shirt.

"Hey." His fingers pressed beneath my chin, forcing my face out of the crook of his neck. "What's this?" He swiped his thumb beneath my eye, wiping my tears away. "Why are you crying, baby?"

I sniffled and pulled in a breath, searching for the

courage to say what needed to be said. There was no more putting it off. It was time.

"I'm really scared."

He looked like I'd just punched him. "Of me?"

Reaching up, I cupped his cheek and shook my head. "No. Never of you. But the way I feel about you terrifies me."

His brows pulled together. "Why?"

It was now or never, so I decided to rip off the Band-Aid, get it over with so I could deal with what came next.

"Because I'm in love with you," I admitted quietly. "I'm in love with you, and you're leaving. And I know that when you do, it's going to crush me."

Tanner's eyes flared wide and his mouth opened to form a perfect O. I sat frozen in his lap as I watched him process what I'd confessed. Then the man did something I wasn't expecting and smiled the most beautiful, brilliant smile I'd ever seen on him.

My face pinched into a frown and I narrowed my eyes, feeling salty all of the sudden. "Why are you smiling? This isn't the time to smile. I poured my guts out to you, and you're smiling like the freaking Joker."

"Are you kidding?" Dear god, he looked downright giddy. "The girl of my dreams just told me she's in love with me, and you expect me not to smile?"

"Wha—"

That was all I got out before he slammed his lips down on mine. The kiss was hungry and possessive. It lit my body up like I was the sky on New Year's Eve, and I was incapable of stopping it.

"Just so you know, I'm in love with you too."

Until that very moment, I didn't realize that words had the power to heal someone completely.

Chapter Twenty-Five

Holiday

I twisted in Tanner's lap, bracing my knees on either side of his hips as I took his face in my hands and crashed my lips against his, pouring every ounce of emotion I was feeling into the kiss. It took no time at all for Tanner to catch up. His hands traveled up my thighs and beneath the dress I'd worn for dinner at the Groves earlier that night.

A trail of goosebumps popped up everywhere he touched, like electricity crawling along my skin. I couldn't get enough of this man, and I wasn't sure I ever would. Or if I even wanted to.

And now that I knew he loved me too . . . everything felt different, like the intensity had been turned up to a million.

He pulled my bottom lip between his teeth and sucked it as his hands grasped my ass. He used his hold on me to rock me against the rigid erection tenting the front of his slacks. A needy moan was wrenched from my throat as his hard length pressed against my clit.

"Tanner," I breathed, dropping my head back as he licked and sucked and kissed across my neck.

"Right here, Sunshine. Tell me what you need."

My hands tangled in his hair as I ground my hips down on him harder, my core aching and desperate to be filled. "You. I want you inside me. Right now."

Tanner bunched the skirt of my dress in his hands, lifting it up and whipping it over my head. My bra came next, leaving me in nothing but a tiny thong. He dragged the tip of his tongue up the straining tendon at the side of my neck before biting the sensitive skin there. "Is that sweet little pussy ready for me?"

"Mmm," I hummed as a rush of arousal flooded my core and drenched my panties. "Always ready for you."

"You know what I want to hear, baby. Give that to me, and I'll give you everything you want. Always will."

I didn't have a doubt about that. He'd proven it time and time again. But this man—*my* man, he wanted to hear me beg for it first. The payoff was more than worth it, so I didn't mind one damn bit.

"Please," I pleaded, my voice coming out high-pitched as the need to come threatened to suck me under and overwhelm every one of my senses. "*Please* fuck me. I need you so bad, I can't stand it."

A wicked smile pulled at his lips, turning me on even more. "Does my good girl want to ride my cock?"

"Yes," I panted, fisting his button-down in my hands. "Take this off. I want to feel you."

Instead of unbuttoning the shirt like I expected, he gripped both sides and tore, sending buttons flying.

My mouth fell open as he stripped it off and tossed it aside like it was nothing. "Oh my god," I breathed, my chest heaving as my heart started to race even faster. "Why the hell was that so hot?"

Tanner cupped me behind the neck with one hand and jerked me back to his mouth, kissing me like his life depended on it as we both fumbled with the button and zipper of his pants.

As soon as his long, thick cock sprang free, I lifted up on my knees. Sliding my panties to the side, I fisted his length at the base and positioned it at my opening before sinking down, taking him all the way inside me.

"*Yes,*" I cried out, throwing my head back as a growl ripped from his throat.

"So goddamn tight. Every time." His hands returned to my ass, lifting me up and slamming me back down as he lifted his hips to meet me, thrusting impossibly deeper. "My Sunshine was made for me," he grunted as we both lost control.

Our movements and kisses were sloppy and uncoordinated as we chased after a release that would likely ruin us both for anyone else. Not that I wanted there to be anyone else. Ever.

Tanner Fine was it for me. I'd heard Gypsy and her friends talk about their epic loves. I'd witnessed my own friends find theirs one by one. I'd started to doubt if I'd ever find one of my own. Then this amazing man crash landed into my life and turned it on its head.

"I love you," I breathed, my lips brushing against his as I rode him so hard and fast a sheen of sweat broke out across my skin.

A primal, animalistic sound rumbled from his chest as he fisted my hair at the base of my neck. "Say it again."

"I love you." The pressure in my core grew and grew as we fucked each other like our lives depended on it. "Tanner, I love you."

"Fuck," he hissed, snapping his hips up again and again. "I'll never get tired of hearing that. Not. Fucking. Ever." Each word was punctuated by a thrust until I teetered right there on the precipice of an orgasm that was so profound, I was actually scared to fall over.

"Give it to me, Sunshine. Let me see all that beauty as you come around me. I want to feel it."

I whimpered, pressing my forehead against his as my pace sped up, my body moving without any input from me as it chased after that release. One of Tanner's hands slid between our bodies, right to where we were connected. The rough pad of his finger pressed against my clit, and that was all it took. Everything exploded in an array of technicolor. Stars burst in front of my eyes as I cried out, clamping down around him as he swelled thicker inside me.

On a rough shout, Tanner followed after me, spilling inside me as he came. What just happened was a first for me, unlike anything I'd ever experienced, and I finally understood the difference between great sex, and amazing sex with a person you loved.

As we both struggled to catch our breaths, Tanner gripped the back of my neck once more, bringing my forehead to his. Those warm amber eyes were on fire as he stared into mine, straight down to my soul.

"You're the love of my life," he whispered, and on that declaration, he mended every single piece of my heart that had ever been broken.

Once we were finally able to move, Tanner lifted me off him with a gentleness that threatened to bring tears to my eyes all over again. He climbed off the couch and moved through the house unabashedly naked. As I watched the taut muscles of his ass flex, I knew I'd never get tired of the sight of my man naked. In fact, I made a promise to myself right then and there to try and make that happen as often as possible.

He cleaned between my legs with a warm wash-cloth, wiping away the remnants of our combined release, and once he was done, he stretched across the length of the couch, pulling me against him so I was lying partially at his side and on his chest. Grabbing the throw blanket, he smoothed it over us, wrapped his arms around me, and settled in.

The silence surrounding us was a comfort, and as the seconds ticked by, I felt my eyelids growing heavy. Then he spoke, and what he said wiped away any and all exhaustion. "I'm not going back."

Stacking my hands on Tanner's rounded pecs, I lifted my head and rested my chin on them so I could see his face. "What?"

"To DC. I'm not going back. I'm retiring. I'm staying here."

My mouth opened but no words came out. It was everything I wanted to hear but it also filled me with guilt at the same time.

"Tanner." I gave him a smile that I hoped didn't look

as sad as it felt. "I can't ask you to do that. Hockey's your life."

"Hockey *was* my life. And you didn't ask. It's a decision I made myself . . . for me." He hooked one arm around my waist and lifted the other, folding it behind his head, causing his bicep to flex. "I've been thinking about retiring for a long time. I'm thirty-seven. Most guys in the league retire before they get to be as old as I am. Especially in my position." He pursed his lips, blowing out a breath as the wheels in his head turned.

I bit down on my bottom lip, hope and concern warring inside of me. "I don't want you to do this for me. You'd end up resenting me, and I don't know if I could handle that."

He smiled softly, the fingers at my back playing with the ends of my loose hair. "I could never resent you. Truth is, my body can't handle it anymore. These couple months in Hope Valley have been the only time in years that I haven't been in pain. I'd like to retire now, before I'm forced out because of an injury I may not bounce back from as quickly. I've had a hell of a career, and two Cups to show for it. I'm good, I swear. I've accomplished everything I've ever wanted to accomplish in the league. Now I'm excited for what comes next. I'm excited for my life *here*. With you." His smile grew as he added, "The woman I love more than life itself."

The wave of emotion that crashed into me was so strong I had to slam my eyes closed and burrow my face into his chest.

"Tell me you want that too, Sunshine." He gave my hair a gentle tug so I'd lift my face back to his. His expression was solemn as he stared down at me. "I think it might actually kill me if you don't."

"I want that," I swore to him. "I want everything with you."

Relief skated over his features. "Good." He hugged me tighter. "Tell me about this place. I know the house up front belongs to your oldest sister, but what's the story with this one?"

A faint smile tugged at my lips as I pulled up some of the happiest memories of my life. "This was Odette's home."

"Odette?"

"She's the closest thing I ever had to a grandmother. Until I was six years old, my siblings and I lived in this dinky, rundown trailer park on the opposite side of town. Odette's trailer was a few doors down from ours." I pulled a fortifying breath into my lungs as I turned my head, resting my cheek on his chest as I braced myself to give him the parts of me I'd been holding back. My parents took off when I was too young to really remember them."

"Jesus," Tanner grunted.

"It wasn't all bad. I mean, it's not like you can miss someone you don't remember. Gypsy was in her early twenties by then, and she'd basically been raising each of us from birth already. She gave up everything to take care of us. She did her absolute best, busted her ass to make sure none of us felt like we were missing out, and we didn't. That's how incredible my big sister is. She filled both roles so well, I sometimes forget they weren't hers from the start."

His voice was jagged as he said, "I love that she gave you that."

"I do too."

"But I hate that you guys had it so hard."

I inhaled deeply. "I do too, especially for her. But she had Odette. We all did. As soon as Detty realized our parents had taken off, she stepped up. She babysat while Gypsy worked two jobs. Any way she could help, she did, until she became as much a part of the family as any of us. When Gypsy met Marco, everything changed. He saved my sister. He saved all of us. He actually bought this house for us. Picked it precisely because it had a second structure on the property that Odette could move into so she could have her own space while still being with her family."

My vision started to grow fuzzy with unshed tears as

I thought about the woman who'd meant so much to me, who'd been such a massive part of my life for so long. "Detty was who I came to when I needed someone who could calm the storm. She was a steadying presence, and she had this way of giving me peace. Aside from my shop, this is the place I come to when I need to feel that. She may be gone, but when I come here, I can still feel her all around me."

"She sounds like an amazing woman."

"She was the best," I said with a wistful smile. "I miss her every single day, but it's not the kind of missing that causes pain, you know? She hadn't been young when she first came into our lives, but we got to keep her for another twenty years, and she kept teaching us new things up until that very last day."

Lifting my head, I propped my chin back on my hands so I could see into Tanner's eyes. "Whenever I felt broken, she put me back together."

"Baby," he breathed, the word coming out pained. "You are not broken."

"I felt like it sometimes. I always swore to myself that I would never *ever* settle for a man like my father. But every man I let into my life managed to turn out just like him. I had a father who couldn't be bothered to love me followed by a string of terrible relationships that chipped away pieces of me. It's hard not to feel broken after something like that."

His hand came up to the side of my neck, his thumb soothingly rubbing along my jaw. "We all break here and there. It's just a part of life. But you kept putting yourself back together. That's what matters. All those beautifully broken pieces were glued back into place, and, baby, they created the most breathtaking mosaic. I see it every time I look at you."

God, the way this man undid me. "Detty would have loved you. I have no doubt she's smiling down on me right now."

"Then I give you my word, right here and now, that I'll strive every single day to be the kind of man she'd want for you."

I didn't doubt that for a single second. And that made me love him even more.

Chapter Twenty-Six

Holiday

"So . . . does this mean you guys are official?"

That question came from Naomi, and was about the hundredth question thrown my way in the past half hour. Not that I minded. I was still riding the high of Tanner and me sharing our *I love yous* the night before.

The grapevine had worked overtime, and word of what had happened at the Tap Room managed to make its way through town, getting back to my friends. By the time I opened One More Chapter, they were already gathered out on the sidewalk, waiting to ambush me.

Between helping customers, I answered every question they threw my way. Well, with the exception of the more personal ones, such as, *How good was the makeup sex once you got everything out on the table?*—of course, that one came from Lennix. I wouldn't have expected any less from my bold, brash bestie.

I couldn't keep the smile off my face as I stood at the front counter, trying and failing to work on the schedule for the following week.

"Yes, we made things official," I answered, rolling my eyes teasingly. Truth was, it felt like a swarm of butterflies had been flapping their wings, creating gale-force winds in my belly since I woke up wrapped in Tanner's arms earlier that morning. I wasn't just happy. I was downright giddy.

"Oh my god, look at her face." Ivy jabbed her finger in my direction, a shit-eating grin tugging at her lips. "I don't think I've ever seen you look this happy."

At the sound of a sniffle, I turned to find Lennix with tears in her eyes. My brows dipped into a frown as I abandoned the schedule and rounded the counter. "What's the matter, babe?"

"Nothing. It's nothing." She waved off my concern. "I'm just really, really happy for you. That's all. You deserve all the good things. Nothing but the good things."

I didn't know what I'd done in a past life to earn the friends I had, but there wasn't a day that went by that I wasn't grateful for each and every one of them. As I pulled my best friend into a tight hug, I had to blink fast against the burn starting behind my own eyes.

I didn't think I had any tears left after the night before—it had been an emotional rollercoaster, to say the least—but apparently I was wrong.

"Have I mentioned lately how much I love you guys?" I looked at the small group that had gathered around me—Lennix, Merritt, Ivy, Rae, and Naomi—and remembered how lucky I was for the support system I had. And the women who were with me were only the tip of the iceberg.

"The feeling is more than mutual," Rae replied from the comforts of the overstuffed chair closest to the register, her feet propped up on the ottoman with a bag of chocolate covered raisins resting on her swollen belly.

Merritt braced her elbow on the counter and rested her chin in her hand. "So where do you guys go from here?"

A blush heated my cheeks as I told them everything Tanner and I had talked about the night before. "Well, he said he's retiring from the league, and he's moving to Hope Valley to be with me."

"Holy shit!" Lennix squealed. She had gotten a handle on her weepiness, and now her eyes were wide and full of something that looked a lot like glee. "Blane is going to lose his *shit*." My friends all burst into laughter.

"I can picture his face when he finally realizes how badly he fucked up. It's only a matter of time before it hits him that he's engaged to a raging harpy, and he'll never have another chance with you because our girl here has leveled way the hell up."

I couldn't lie, I kind of liked that idea myself.

"We talked a bit about what he wants to do after his retirement, and he's thinking about coaching. There's a youth league in this county, and he likes the idea of helping little kids discover their love of the game the same way he did."

I went on to tell them about his mom and his former coach, and there was more than a little swooning happening in the shop. And I was right there with them.

They hung around a while longer, sharing in the happiness that was swelling so big inside of me that I wasn't sure I'd be able to contain it. They finally left a little while later, and I spent the rest of the day moving through the shop like I was floating on air. I was in such a good mood, I didn't think it was possible for anything to bring me down.

I should have known there was another shoe hovering above me, waiting to drop.

The worst thing about it was that the blow came from the one woman who was supposed to have loved me and my siblings above all else.

I'd made it through most of the day without thinking about her. That dark, miserable cloud was always hovering in the background, waiting to cast a shadow on the life I'd built for myself.

The texts started coming in. Picture after picture of Tanner and me together. Having lunch at the diner. Walking hand in hand out of Muffin Top. There were even pictures of us inside the Tap Room. I didn't know if she'd been the one to take them or if it had been the asshole who trashed my apartment all those weeks ago, but as I scrolled through them, a slimy chill slithered down my spine. Because I knew what was coming.

Sure enough, there was a message that followed the photos, and what it said chilled me to my bones.

See you landed yourself a whale. Now I know you got money. Two hundred grand, or I sell these pictures to whichever gossip site's willing to pay the most.

My lungs squeezed tighter as I read the words over and over. I remembered everything Tanner said about the people in his past who only came into his life because they wanted to use him for his money and fame. Even his own father. And I refused to let my mother do the same thing.

With shaking hands, I stuffed the phone in my back pocket and grabbed my purse from under the counter.

"Denise, would you mind covering for the rest of the day? Something's come up that I need to take care of."

My manager looked at me, her brows pinching with concern as soon as she caught the look on my face. "Of course. Do what you have to do. We'll take care of things."

I shot her a grateful smile, then hustled out of the shop. My mind ran through a thousand different scenarios of how Tanner was going to handle the fact that I'd been keeping this secret, and none of them ended happily.

My stomach was in knots and my heart was racing when I pulled up to the cabin. Tanner must have heard my car coming up the drive because he was already standing on the porch as I climbed the front steps. The smile on his face slowly melted when he caught sight of my expression.

He moved to me, taking my face in his hands. "What's wrong?" His brows slammed together, worry filling his eyes. "Is it another migraine?"

I shook my head. "No, it's not that." I swallowed, trying to soothe the sudden dryness in my throat. "Can we go inside? There's something I need to tell you."

I couldn't sit still. I paced the length of the living room as Tanner read through all the texts between me and my mother. The silence filling the cabin was slowly suffocating me, and with each second that ticked by, the anxiety tightening my muscles grew worse. By the time he finally looked up at me from his place on the couch, it felt like an eternity had passed.

"I'm so sorry." The words spilled out without any prompting from my brain. "I should have told you about this from the very beginning. Or at least once you told me about your father. I wasn't trying to keep secrets from you. I just . . ." I had to stop, the lump forming in my throat making it hard to speak and even harder to breathe. A burn of tears wanted to come, and I struggled to keep them at bay. Shame washed over me, coating my skin like a sticky film as I dropped my gaze to my feet, unable to meet his eyes.

"I didn't want you to know that was the kind of person I came from. I didn't want you to think less of me," I finally admitted, speaking my worst fear out loud for the very first time. The words came out rough and jagged, like they were being ripped from my throat.

For such a big guy, he moved with surprising stealth. One second he was on the couch, and the next he was standing right in front of me. The feel of his fingers beneath my chin gave me a jolt, and I jerked my gaze up to meet his.

"Sunshine." A smiled spread across his face, and at the sight of it, I took my first full breath since that text came through. "There's nothing you could do or say that would ever make me think less of you."

My lips parted, forming an O as his words slipped over me, fighting away that chill that had stuck to me like a splinter beneath my skin since I left the shop. "You can't know that for sure." My chest expanded on a deep inhale. "Tanner, this is something that keeps following me around, dogging every step I take. Just when I start to settle and lower my guard, she pops up from whatever hole she lives in to remind me there's no escape. She's never going away." I shook my head sadly. "I can't ask you to take that on."

He caressed my neck in that way I loved, the way that made me feel so damn safe. "You don't have to ask me. I'm doing it anyway."

My eyes flared wide as panic set it. "Tanner, no. You can't do that. If you pay her, she'll never leave you alone.

She's a goddamn leach. The worst kind of bottom feeder there is. She found out I was with you and all she saw was dollar signs."

His expression never changed, never wavered. "Last night changed everything," he stated. "As far as I'm concerned you belong to me as much as I belong to you, and I take care of what's mine." His thumb brushed against my jaw. "I get that you felt you needed to carry this burden on your own to protect your family, but we're a team now. It's you and me. And I'll be damned if I stand by and watch as someone tries to take advantage of you." He pulled in a deep breath, determination etched onto every inch of his face as he said, "I have a plan."

My tongue came out, swiping across my bottom lip nervously as I nodded in agreement. I didn't know what his plan was, and I didn't need to. I trusted the man in front of me with everything in me. Most especially my heart. "What do you want to do?"

"Well, you aren't going to like it, but it starts with you telling your siblings what's been going on." He arched a brow, that dominant expression that was usually reserved for the bedroom taking over. "No more secrets. We're getting this out in the open. Today."

Oh hell.

Chapter Twenty-Seven

Tanner

To say the past hour and a half had been rough would have been the understatement of the century. After our talk, Holly had texted her family, asking them to meet us at the cabin. Once they arrived she dove right in, confessing everything she'd been keeping to herself for the better part of a year. How their mother had reached out to demand money. How she'd continued to pay, even going so far as to drain her savings to keep that vile woman satisfied so she wouldn't go after her siblings.

As hard as it was, I had to sit back and let her handle it, offering my silent support as Holly admitted her mistakes to the people she loved most in the world. As much as I wanted to take on the weight that had been loaded onto her shoulders, that was the part she had to take care of herself. And she was. Despite everything, she showed a strength that left me in awe of her. I'd never met someone as resilient as Holiday Bradbury, and witnessing it first-hand only made me love her more.

The emotions that filled the cabin like dense fog ran the gamut from anger—her brothers—all the way to sadness—from her sisters, Sunny and Gypsy.

At one point, I nearly lost my grip on the self-control I was struggling to hold on to. It had taken everything in me to keep from jumping in and punching Raylan in the face when he let his anger fly, snapping at Holly in a tone that had me curling my hands into fists so tight I thought the skin around my knuckles would split open.

The man in question paced the room like a caged lion. "Just when I think those fuckers are gone from our lives for good, they pop up like fucking cockroaches." He pinned Holly in place with a furious glare. "I can't believe you've been keeping this to yourself. I can't believe you gave that bitch money! What were you thinking?"

That was the last straw.

"That's enough." The room went silent at the bass of my voice, seven sets of eyes landing on and following me as I moved to Holly, wrapping my arms around her waist and pulling her into my side. She sniffled and tried to be discreet as she wiped her eyes, but I didn't miss the dampness that clung to her lashes. This was costing her. And she was done paying the price alone.

"I understand you're angry." I looked directly at Raylan. "All of you have every right to be. But you need to direct that anger at the correct target, and that's not your sister."

I felt eyes on me coming from the corner of the room near the fireplace, and when I looked over I found Marco, standing sentry, ready to jump in and protect at any moment. He's been quiet the whole time, observing. But as his hazel eyes locked on me, I saw appreciation in them. He dipped his chin, and something that felt a hell of a lot like pride made my chest swell. That man had been the first line of defense for the Bradbury siblings for years, and I got the sense he was accepting that I was now there to stand beside him, offering even more protection.

Raylan's expression shifted from anger to remorse. "I'm sorry, sweetheart," he said softly. "I hate the thought that you've been alone in this."

"I wanted to protect you," Holly replied, her voice wavering slightly. "The way you guys have always protected me." Her eyes landed on each of her brothers and sisters. "You guys fought to find your happiness.

You've found your partners and started families of your own, and I didn't want her to take that away."

"We're stronger together."

That came from Gypsy. She was the closest thing their family had to a matriarch, and when she talked everyone listened. She'd sacrificed everything for her siblings without a second thought, and from the look on her face, I knew she'd have gladly done it over and over again.

"That's the one thing about this family that's always been true. We're stronger together. We're a team." She stood from the couch and walked over to her youngest sister. "I love you, and I appreciate you wanting to protect us all by yourself, but that's not how we work. We take on the worst as a whole. That's how we win. You understand me?"

Holly's throat bobbed on a swallow as she nodded. "I understand."

Gypsy inhaled, resoluteness steeling her spine, and as I watched her put herself back together, I finally understood where Holly got her strength. "All right, then. Now that that's settled we need to figure out what we're going to do."

I gave Holly a squeeze, looking down at her and silently communicating to make sure we were on the same page. When she nodded, I spoke up. "If you guys agree, I'm pretty sure I know how to take care of this situation once and for all."

Gypsy's head twisted in my direction, and when her eyes met mine, I saw acceptance, clear as day. "What do you have in mind?"

"I want Holly to text her back. Tell her you have the money and that you want to meet up."

"You think that's a good idea?" Sunny asked, her expression fierce. "I don't want Holly to have to face that woman."

"She won't be. Holly's staying here, I'm the one who's going to face her."

"I'm going with you," Raylan declared.

Holly's youngest brother Lee pushed out of the chair he'd been sitting in. "Me too."

"Oh, there's no way in hell I'm missing this," Rhodes added.

I nodded in agreement. If they wanted to watch as I made sure Peggy Bradbury never darkened their doorsteps again, that was fine with me.

THE ROADSIDE MOTEL thirty minutes outside of Hope Valley where Holly's mother was staying looked like it should have been condemned years ago. We drove past a drug deal in progress as I guided my Range Rover into a parking spot, and a few yards away, a woman I was fairly certain was a prostitute was leading a man into one of the other rooms.

"Christ, this place is a goddamn dump," Rhodes grunted from the passenger seat. "Could probably get hepatitis just by touching any surface."

As I killed the engine, the door to the room directly in front of us opened and a woman who looked at least a decade and a half older than she actually was stepped outside. She tucked a cigarette between her lips and lit it up, staring at us through the windshield.

"That's her." I looked over at Rhodes as he glared at the woman, the muscle in his jaw ticking as he clenched his teeth together.

"Jesus." Lee's lip curled up in disgust. "I can't believe that's the woman we came from."

"Neither can I," Raylan muttered, letting out a resigned sigh. "We've already been here longer than I want to be. Let's get this shit over with."

We climbed out of the car, and as I rounded the hood, I kept my eyes locked on the woman who looked like life had chewed her up and spit her out. I couldn't help but wonder what was so tempting about the way she was living that she'd choose it over her own children. There wasn't a doubt in my mind that Holly and her siblings were better off without her.

As her gaze bounced over her sons, I wondered if she realized that she'd have been better off if she stayed. In the end, it didn't matter, though. Because they had managed to thrive without her.

"That's one fancy-ass ride you got there," she said to me, blowing out a puff of noxious smoke through her stained teeth. "You obviously got some money to throw around."

I didn't bother denying it. "That I do. A whole lot of it, actually."

She looked over my shoulder, and for a brief moment I thought I caught a flash of sorrow in her eyes as she looked at her sons, but it was there and gone before I could be sure. "And I see you brought my sons with you." She sneered, turning her attention back to me. "What? You afraid you needed backup or somethin'?"

"We aren't your sons," Rhodes stated definitively. "You don't have any sons or daughters. You're all alone, Peggy."

That flash returned, and I watched as she shook it off, taking another puff of her cigarette. She was trying to play it off that she didn't care, but it didn't work. That blow from Rhodes had landed, and it did some real damage. "I didn't agree to no family reunion. I got shit to do, so just give me my money, and you can be on your way."

My lips curled up in a smile that felt downright feral as I pulled the check out of my pocket and handed it over.

She snatched it out of my had, greed carved into every line on her face. At least until she unfolded it and saw the amount.

"The fuck is this?" she demanded, waving the check in the air.

"That's a thousand dollars," I stated simply.

Her cheeks grew red with anger. "This some kind of fuckin' joke? You tryin' to play me? I said two hundred grand."

I took a step closer. I wasn't above using my size to intimidate when the situation called for it. And in this case, it was definitely called for. Whatever she saw on my face made her step back. Her bravado fell away, replaced with uncertainty and a little bit of fear.

"That's all you're going to get. Ever. I came here to tell you that your well's dried up."

Her face pinched up in a glare. She was trying to come off as threatening, but she only looked pathetic.

"That's not how this works. You give me what I want, or I'll make your life miserable. You hear me?"

I wasn't sure I'd ever hated anyone before, but looking at Peggy Bradbury, I knew without a shadow of a doubt that I hated this woman. "That thousand dollars is the last you'll ever see from any person with the last name Bradbury," I gritted through clenched teeth. "I came here today to tell you that you just played your last card. And you lost. You fucked up when you decided to threaten my woman."

I moved closer, the blood in my veins reaching a full boil. "I protect the people I care about. That check you have in your hand right now is barely a drop in the bucket for me. I have *millions*. More than you could ever dream of having, and if you come anywhere near Holly or her siblings ever again, if you reach out in any way, I will use every goddamn dime I have to my name to destroy what little you have left of your pathetic life."

I curled my lips, baring my teeth. "I will make sure every single day of your sad existence is a misery. The difference between me and you, I have the means to back up my threats. You want to test me on that? Fuck around and find out. I actually think I'd enjoy ruining you."

Her body was shaking so bad I thought her knees were going to give out, but somehow she managed to stay standing. "What happens now is you're going to disappear. You're going to get as far away from Hope Valley as that thousand will take you, and you're going to forget any of these people exist. Do *you* hear *me?*" I hissed, throwing her own words back at her.

She swallowed thickly as her head moved in a jerky nod.

"Good." I started to turn but stopped to issue one more warning. "Lose Holly's number. If you don't there isn't a corner of this planet you could hide in that I wouldn't find you."

With that, I turned on my heel and stomped back toward the car. Rhodes was standing stoic but there was no missing the respect in his eyes. Lee gaped at me before letting out a full-blown laugh. Finally, I looked at Raylan to find him grinning at me, ear to ear.

He reached out and clapped me on the shoulder. "That was something, man. All I can say after witnessing that is, welcome to the family, brother."

The only sweeter words I'd ever heard was when Holly told me she loved me. "Glad to hear it. Now let's get the hell out of here."

Epilogue

Holiday

S*ummer*

"That's the last of it."

I turned away from the amazing views outside my new living room window and smiled at Tanner as he set the box of books on the floor by the built-in bookshelves.

My eyes widened in surprise. "That's everything out of the truck?"

Tanner let out a snort. "Hell no. I just meant that's the last of the books."

Between the two of us, we had enough books to make a library of our very own, and as I stared at the boxes, I couldn't help but think about which room I wanted to convert.

A lot had happened over the past several months. The owners of the cabin Tanner had been renting accepted his offer, and then as soon as the ink dried on the papers, he asked me to move in with him. It had been a no-brainer. Sure, I loved my little apartment above One More Chapter, and the commute couldn't be beat, but the cabin in the woods somehow managed to be grand and cozy at the same time; it was the kind of house I'd only dreamed of living in.

I wanted to make it a home for both of us, and—fingers crossed—maybe our own family one day. But those were thoughts for further into the future.

Tanner was officially retired from the NHL and was already in talks with the youth league about coaching. They'd tripped over themselves to say yes when he inquired. I mean, what could be better than having a two-time Stanley Cup winner as a coach?

Since Tanner's showdown with our mother, I hadn't heard a peep from her, and I couldn't find it in me to be sad about that. I didn't need her in my life, not when it was already so full of people who loved and supported me.

"Jesus, will you quit slacking off and help me get this damn thing through the door?"

"I am helping!"

I turned just as Tanner's former teammates and friends, Caleb and Mateo maneuvered one half of a large sectional into the living room.

With it being summer, the hockey season was officially over, so Tanner's friends had agreed to help with the move. Tanner headed back to DC for a few days to pack up the rest of his apartment, and the three of them, plus Luke, made the trip to Hope Valley to help their friend settle into his new home. Where Luke was a solid, stable presence, Caleb and Mateo were hilarious chaos.

It was easy to see why the four of them were as close as they were, and I loved that my man had that close circle of friends that were more like family.

"You are not," Mateo snapped. "Lift with your legs, you lazy bastard."

"I've got my end, you're the lazy bastard," Caleb gritted through clenched teeth and he shifted his hold on his end of the couch. "We get back to DC, I'm gonna beat your ass."

I tried to cover my laugh with a cough and failed miserably.

"Language!"

The sharp reprimand was followed by Tanner's mother entering the room, carrying a floor lamp in one hand and Yoda in the other.

Tanner's mother, Elaine, and step-father, Andrew, had come to Hope Valley for a visit not long after Tanner took care of everything with Peggy, and it took no time at all for me to fall in love with the woman. She was smart and sassy and hilarious. She had her husband wrapped around her little finger, and watching the two of them together made me excited for the future I'd have with Tanner.

I wasn't the only one who'd taken a liking to the woman who was responsible for raising the most amazing man in the world. Yoda had developed a crush in no time, and I was starting to think that my cat liked her more than me.

"Sorry," the two grown ass men mumbled like they were school children being lectured by a teacher.

Elaine caught my eye and winked, her eyes—the very same eyes as Tanner—glittered with humor.

Tanner rushed over to help before the two of them broke something, and I left them to the heavy lifting as I headed to the kitchen.

It wasn't just Tanner's friends helping us to set up our new life. My family was also there, along with my whole circle of friends.

Tristan and Merritt were out back, keeping an eye on her nephews, Levi and Toby, as they explored the property around the cabin. Rhodes and Blythe had brought enough pizza to feed an army. Rae was kicked back on one of the Adirondak chairs on the front porch, enjoying the sun and shouting orders at Zach as she cradled their precious baby girl, Ellie, against her chest. Connor and Raylan were helping unload the rest of our things with Andrew, Lee, and Marco, while my sisters, Lennix, and Naomi were in the kitchen, unpacking the bazillion boxes of dishes and appliances.

As I stood in the middle of the open space, taking in the fact that everyone I loved was here with me, a warmth unlike anything I'd ever experienced filled my chest and spread out into my limbs. This was what I'd been looking for my whole life. What I'd started to think wasn't meant for me.

Until I met a man who gave me my *everything*.

Tanner caught me watching him, a smile playing across his lips as he moved in my direction. Just like always, as soon as he was close enough, he grabbed me around the waist and pulled me into his chest.

"What's on your mind, Sunshine?

I shrugged my shoulders as I rested my palms on his chest. Tilting my head back, I smiled up at the man I loved with every single beautifully broken piece of me. When he cupped the side of my neck, I leaned into his touch. "I was just thinking about how lucky I am."

His expression turned tender. "Is that right?"

"Yeah. I have my family, my friends, and the man I love all under one roof. I don't think there's anything better than that."

Tanner let out a hum of mock thought. "See, I'm not so sure about that." I arched a brow in question. "I think it actually *could* get better. But that depends on one thing."

"Yeah? What's that?"

He reached into his pocket and pulled out the most beautiful ring I'd ever seen as he lowered onto one knee. The breath whooshed from my lungs, and I vaguely noticed everyone had gathered around. I felt them watching us, but I couldn't take my eyes off the man kneeling in front of me.

"When I was injured, I thought I lost everything, that my life was over. What I didn't realize was that it was only getting started. The moment I walked into your bookstore, you lit up my entire world. You are my new beginning, and I want nothing more than for you to be my ending as well. So, Holiday Bradbury, will you make me the happiest man on earth and be my wife?"

"Yes," I said on a single breath. the smile wreathing my face was so big my cheeks hurt. "Yes!" I repeated on a shout. Tanner shot to his feet and scooped me up, spinning me in a circle as I laughed and everyone who loved us cheered for the next chapter we were about to start.

When he finally put me down, he slid the ring onto my finger and sealed my lips with his, pouring every ounce of love he had for me into that kiss.

He pulled away enough to rest his forehead against mine. "You ready to start forever with me, baby?"

I grinned up at my future husband. "I can't wait."

The End.

Thank you so much for for reading Tanner and Holly's story. I hope you enjoyed the ride!

If you're curious about Gypsy and Marco's story, or want to learn more about the beloved Odette, check out ***Wrong Side of the Tracks***.

AVAILABLE FOR PURCHASE OR IN KU HERE

About Jessica

Born and raised around Houston, Jessica is a self proclaimed caffeine addict, connoisseur of inexpensive wine, and the worst driver in the state of Texas. In addition to being all of these things, she's first and foremost a wife and mom.

Growing up, she shared her mom and grandmother's

love of reading. But where they leaned toward murder mysteries, Jessica was obsessed with all things romance.

When she's not nose deep in her next manuscript, you can usually find her with her kindle in hand.